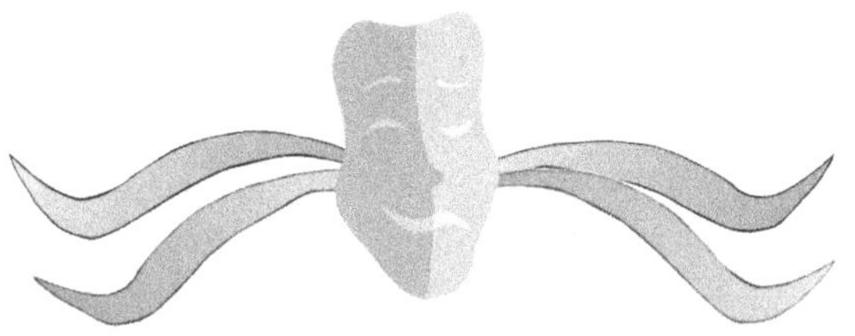

Thony winced.

**"<u>NOT</u>. I'm not <u>interested</u> in anyone, guy <u>or</u> girl.
I don't have the <u>right</u> to be <u>interested</u>," he began.**

"Your Big Quest, yadda, yadda, yadda," Daffyd rolled his eyes. "It's to find someone to marry you, right?"

"A *princess*," Thony clarified. "Whose *dad* will lend me his *army* to protect Aldyrwald."

"*Someone*," Daffyd corrected. "And how much of an 'army' do you need anyways? A dozen knights and maybe a couple hundred regular troops? Or the equivalent?"

Thony blinked. He hadn't actually thought about *numbers*.

"About that, I suppose," he admitted, after thinking about it for a moment. "More wouldn't hurt, though."

It wasn't likely there was anyone in the Mountain-Region who would know how to manage terribly large forces.

"You think too much," Daffyd said as Thony ruminated on these new ideas.

And then Thony found himself being kissed without asking. *Again.*

And it was still the same problem. He didn't want to *hurt* Daffyd. He just wanted to be *asked*.

(Well, and for his 'no' to be properly respected.)

A COURT OF MISTS AND MISADVENTURES

*Book Six of the
Prankster Prince*

(Book Two of the Pathremiri Problem)

MANGALA MCNAMARA

RISING DRAGON BOOKS

Mangala McNamara

This book is a work of fiction. Names, characters, places, and incidents are the product of the author's imagination or are used fictitiously. Any resemblance to actual events, places or people, living or dead, is coincidental. Made BY humans and FOR humans.

Also available in eBook and paperback editions.
McNamara, Mangala
A Court of Mists and Misadventures by Mangala McNamara Indiana:
Rising Dragon Books, 2025
 p. 1 map
(McNamara, Mangala. The Prankster Prince; bk. 6)
Summary: Prince Thony has quickly realized that Amanita's homeland is not where he needs to be – but the matriarchy doesn't want to let him go. So, he has to run away again, this time taking Amanita's brother, Prince Daffyd with him, and heading to the Land of Snow-Fairies, where Puck's mom is the Queen… and a Goddess…

ISBN 978-1-960160-56-0 (pbk)
1. Princes and princesses - Fiction. 2. Adolescent Rebellion - Fiction
ISBN 978-1-960160-57-7 (hc) ISBN 978-1-960160-55-3 (eBook)

Excerpt from: *Thony and the Much-Anticipated Adventure*
Copyright © 2023 by Mangala McNamara

A Court of Mists and Misadventures: Book 6 of the Prankster Prince (Book Two of the Pathremiri Problem)
Copyright © 2025 by Mangala McNamara
Cover art and illustrations by the author
The Rising Dragon Logo was designed by Priyadevi McNamara
All rights reserved. No part of this book may be reproduced in any format, print or electronic, without permission in writing from the copyright holders.
For further information, email RisingDragonBooks@gmail.com

ISBN: 978-1-960160-56-0
First Print Edition: March 2025
10 9 8 7 6 5 4 3 2 1

To all the kids who just won't stop growing up...
in their own unique ways...
but who aren't necessarily ready to
be grown-ups.

CONTENTS

And for your delectation, an excerpt from...

Thony and the Much-Anticipated Adventure

Book One of the Prankster Prince

THONY
and the Much-Anticipated
Adventure
Book One
of the
Prankster Prince
MANGALA McNAMARA

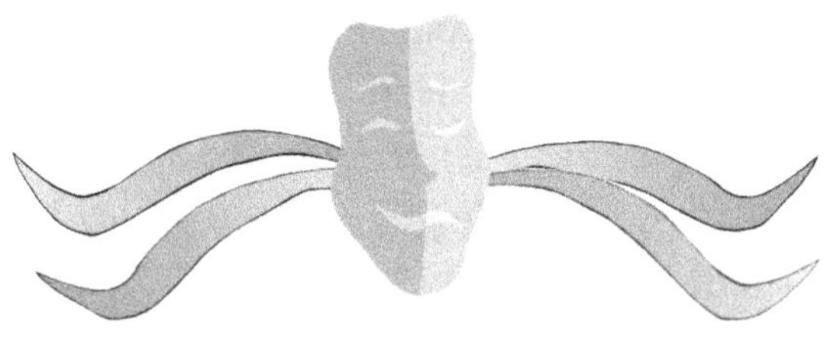

Prologue

(a recap of Pathremir's history as we know it
– according to Thony))

THE FABLED LAND OF PATHREMIR – whose name means *Vengeance* in their most ancient tongue – sits high in the Misty Mountains on a broad plateau.

In the very long distant past, the Pathremiri claim to be descended of dragons and Mist-Maidens *(which are apparently some kind of fairy-people and are **also** known as 'Snow-Fairies')*. Supposedly they were super-chill back then. No wars, no fighting at all, just small family-groups that stayed by themselves and only got together to hang out for major festivals.

They called the place the Land of Mists, maybe because it was actually mistier than it is now or maybe because of those Mist-Maidens who were their ancestors. Or maybe both.

In the not-quite-so-distant past *(like, three thousand years ago)* the ancient Pathremiri people welcomed a bunch of refugee strangers into their land. Sometime thereafter *(either months or years, or possibly even **decades**, depending on whom you talk to)* the refugees – who called themselves the *Líonar* – took over and turned the original Pathremiri people into thralls *(which seems to be their word for **seriously downtrodden peasants**).*

They named the land *Loptheim,* which means 'Land of Clouds' in their language. *(Or maybe 'Land of Mists.')* And they introduced agriculture and drained some swamps and stuff, which might be why it's not all that 'misty' anymore.

There also weren't a great number of these refugee types around, and possibly not a great many of the original Pathremiri people either. So, everybody got all mixed up together. Weirdly, both sides seemed to kind of make almost a religion out of *not* being kin to the other ones, although that probably isn't likely to be true for anybody by now.

After about a thousand years of being thralls, the original Pathremiri people *(or at least the thralls who were more descended of those people than of the Líonar)* got their act together and managed to throw out the 'invaders.' *(A little hard to still call people who've been living there for a thousand years 'invaders'...)*

Most of the Líonar-types went east and mixed it up with the people living down on the coast. Those people were more organized and ready for it *(apparently, they'd been paying attention to the politics next door).* Instead of being conquered by force, they sort of mixed it up on purpose, even though the Líonar-types managed to take over the upper echelons of society there, too.

(Well, sort of managed to. There seems to be a different viewpoint from the descendants of those other people.)

That country to the east is called Selavan.

A small number of the Líonar-types fled to the west instead. That included their king and his sons. The older son apparently died while helping his father and younger brother – and a number of their people – escape.

The king and his younger son – who was now his Heir – settled down just over the peaks that surround the Pathremiri plateau and supposedly spent the rest of his life pining for his wife and daughters. *(Who had been the ones to lead the uprising and overthrow him...)* He and his people never really went very far away, and eventually established themselves on the west side of the mountains, with the stated ambition of returning 'home' to 'Loptheim.'

Which made for some rather tricky relations with the newly-named 'Pathremir.'

They called their 'temporary' residence on the mountainside 'Mountainmeadow' *(possibly because that's all that it was)* and spent the next thousand years trying to come back. *(Or possibly the entire last two thousand years. Again, it depends on whom you talk to.)* Eventually, however, they kind of gave up and became part of a larger kingdom called 'Dawil,' farther to the west and down on some plains.

Oh, and there are these little groups of people living at the very highest-but-still-livable places on the actual mountain peaks. They're supposed to be mostly Líonar-types, though they apparently keep inter-marrying with the people down on the Pathremir plateau, so they're maybe not exactly Líonar. It seems like it's mostly the women in these 'clan-enclaves' marrying Pathremiri *guys*, who are probably pretty relieved to get out of the rather extreme matriarchy of Pathremir.

The 'clan-enclaves' are run by seeresses – women who can magickally see the future – so it's still matriarchal, but it can't possibly be as extreme as in Pathremir, where they flipped the extreme patriarchy that the Líonar had setup on its head and guys aren't allowed to do hardly *anything* without a woman supervising.

There's trade between all these places – Pathremir, Selavan, and Dawil *(or Mountainmeadow)*. And there's a famous university on the border between Dawil and Pathremir, which means even more people passing through. But otherwise, the three places seem to try to ignore each other as much as possible...

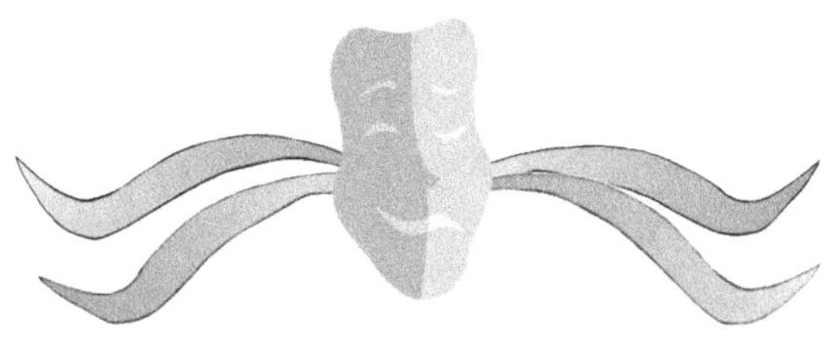

Chapter ONE

Relatively Simple Problems

"I THOUGHT HE CALLED ME and Daffyd his *niece* and *nephew,*" Amanita grumped over breakfast.

Thony was already regretting agreeing to eat with her instead of in his rooms.

But he was trying to be a supportive friend, so...

"Did you get *any* sleep last night?" he asked.

The girl shrugged. "Not much. Vathir made me go to bed eventually – I think he made Môthir go to bed, too. Which left all my *grandparents* still talking or... *whatever.*"

She winced.

Thony rolled his eyes, but he tried not to let his friend see.

They'd arrived in the Queen's City – the capitol of Pathremir – yesterday. The night before they'd stayed at an inn just outside the city so that a Proper Triumphal Return of the Lost Princess could be orchestrated. Puck had – wisely, Thony had thought at the time and with a certain wistful jealousy – made himself scarce to avoid going through the nonsense.

They'd had a huge military escort *(all made up of those short, dark, fierce-looking women – though Thony had been told men were allowed to serve… just not in ceremonial duties nor were they promoted past a certain rank)*.

People *(women and girls, with a few guys way far back)* had actually *lined the streets* to wave little Pathremiri flags and cheer for Amanita.

And somebody had gone all-out and decided to include *trumpets*.

There had been a big, fancy, formal greeting by Queen Namarina *(Amanita and Daffyd's grandmother)*, Princess-Heir Ytheril and Prince-Consort Naeel *(their parents)*, and Eldest-Princess Reyalla *(their other grandmother)*.

And then they had all gone inside the palace. Well, the travelers had, not the adoring crowds or most of the girl-guards.

There had been time for some recriminations *(from the Eldest-Princess; the rest of Amanita and Daffyd's family seemed pretty cool)* and to freshen up before dinner.

And dinner was where it had gotten a little crazy.

The Eldest-Princess had gotten snotty about how they'd stopped Valderon Raven'sWing's war with pranks. Okay, not *exactly* with pranks, but by convincing a lot of people that pranks could *maybe* actually work to do that… which had made Puck – who had turned out to be the honest-to-goodness *demi*-God of Pranks and Mischief – strong enough to break Raven'sWing's spell blocking the Fairy Wood. And then Puck had let Lady Opalsinger and Lord Aspenheart and the other elves free to take out Shalladra Stillheart, the miscreant Dark-elf who was at the root of all the problems.

Eldest-Princess Reyalla hadn't believed any of it.

Daffyd had gotten sick of his grandmother **(that** grandmother, not the Queen) dissing their story, and he'd inadvertently summoned Puck.

None of them had known that Puck could be summoned by saying his name three times in a row.

Also, none of them – including Princess-Heir Ytheril – had known that the Princess-Heir's *father* was *Puck*. Who was better known around here as 'Prince Skiftglow' – the son of Queen Snowmistral of the Snow-Fairies... Who just happened to also be the Goddess Sylphara of the Mountain-Breezes, the 'Lady of Blizzards and Gales.'

It was complicated, for sure. Thony had ended up drawing a bunch of charts in his journal last night to try to keep track of all this stuff: who was related to whom and how.

Apparently, Pathremiri Queens and Princesses didn't need to get married in order for their kids to be legit and all. Or even say who the father of their kids *was.*

All that extreme matriarchy stuff, Thony supposed. Which sort of made a certain amount of sense. After all, if women ruled and guys didn't matter, why worry about it? You could always tell who a baby's *mother* was.

Not that he'd mention that to Amanita.

She'd get that smug look of hers and probably start pontificating at him about how their system was *so superior.*

And right now, he really *was* just trying to be a good friend.

It was probably pretty weird to discover that one of your best friends was also your grandfather.

And Puck didn't look *old enough* to be anyone's dad, let alone *grand*father. Presumably that was because he was a Snow-Fairy. Or a demi-God.

Not that Queen Namarina looked old enough to be anyone's grandma either. She looked about as old as Thony's Mama, who was about forty.

*(Which was **old**, and even 'grandma old' when he stopped to think about it. Papa had 'rescued' Mama when she was sixteen, as was proper. Joanna had turned up shortly thereafter. If Prissy hadn't been born with the bushy, black tail, Joanna would have been 'rescued' and married at sixteen as well, so... Mama would have had at least one grandchild by now. Probably more, since Jo would have been married eight or nine years by now. Whoa.)*

Anyways, when Puck appeared, Queen Namarina and he had got all ooey-gooey and started kissing each other.

It was... a little embarrassing, to be honest.

Daffyd and Thony had booked it after they finished their dinners. Amanita and her mom and her other grandmother (the Eldest-Princess) were all arguing – it wasn't clear with *whom*, since Puck and the Queen had been ignoring all of them. Amanita and Daffyd's dad had gotten stuck sitting there in the middle of it all, but he'd indicated to the boys that *they* could go.

There were some other advantages to a matriarchy – or being a guest. They neither needed nor wanted either of the boys there, so *they* had gotten some sleep.

Or at least Thony had, after he'd stayed up a while writing and drawing those charts. He had no idea what Daffyd had done after they'd parted ways. Since the Pathremiri prince hadn't shown up for breakfast, it was possible he'd stayed up all night stewing, too.

Amanita was still looking sour. And like she expected a response.

"Does it bother you?" Thony asked her. "Puck being your grandfather, I mean."

She shrugged and looked away. "I don't know. Not really, I guess. And I suppose it explains why Môthir doesn't really look like anyone else. She doesn't really look Líonar, but... everyone always sort of assumed she was a... a *throwback*. Because, like Kyrista and Inga mentioned back in Selavan," she added with an unhappy look, "we *do* have Líonar blood in our family. Even if it's all the way back to Queen Varella's daughters."

And various people had mentioned that no one took the quiet Princess-Heir very seriously.

Thony supposed that looking like you were a member of the group everyone hated... wouldn't do you a lot of favors. Considering that *he* seemed to be getting the side-eye from people around here – though it could be because he'd shown up with Amanita, rather than because he was pale and red-headed with blue eyes – he could totally sympathize with Princess Ytheril's situation.

Or with Amanita's, as Ytheril's daughter.

He gave his friend a sympathetic look. "Would this 'everyone' have mostly been your *other* grandmother?"

Amanita made a face. "I wish. No, she's awful, but it really was *everyone* everyone." The girl sighed. "Well, at least one good thing will come of this. If Puck will stick around as *Prince Skiftglow* for awhile and let everyone see him and my Grandmother-the-Queen together, it'll be obvious that Môthir looks like a *Snow-Fairy*. And that's a respectable lineage to anyone and everyone."

"Though we may have to remind everyone that Snow-Fairies are Mist-Maidens." Daffyd had just come into the breakfast room.

He was rubbing a hand through his hair and looking sleepy, but his clothes looked neat. A little snug here and there and short at the cuffs, but otherwise they were starched and pressed everything. And they didn't look like any of the things Thony had seen him wearing the last couple of months.

Thony assumed these were clothes that had been left here when the Pathremiri prince went looking for his little sister and that he'd grown in the intervening months. Daffyd had sort of hunched a bit during all the introductions yesterday as if trying to hide the change in his height.

Amanita glared at him, then wilted a bit and nodded as Daffyd sat down. "Yeah. I don't imagine everyone *else* has their nose rubbed in our history all the time, like we do."

So, the common people of Pathremir weren't as vengeance-obsessed as their undersized princess? That was interesting to know.

"Get a good night's sleep in your own bed?" Thony asked his friend with a touch of envy. He missed his *own* bed in his *own* room back home in Aldyrwald rather more than he would like to admit.

Daffyd shrugged as a servant brought him over a laden plate of food. He thanked the woman politely before answering. "Sort of. I mean, we don't usually spend that much time here, so this isn't the room – or the bed – I'm most used to."

Thony raised his eyebrows. "You don't live in the palace most of the time?"

Daffyd shook his head and pointed to Amanita with his fork as he chewed on a piece of bacon. He was late enough to the meal that the bacon had chilled down from perfectly crispy to slightly leathery. It still tasted good, though.

"We – Daffyd, Vathir, Môthir, and I – live mostly at an estate outside the city. It's only about an hour's ride – Môthir has to go back and forth pretty regularly after all – but it's far enough that we don't have to deal with... certain people all the time." Amanita made another face.

That seemed a little weird to Thony. There had never been a question that Joanna and Roger – and eventually Thony and his bride – would live in Castle Devinthal with Mama and Papa. Prissy and Jeremy only lived outside the castle because Jeremy was a centaur; his sister kept rooms in the castle still, to store her gowns and princessy things.

On the other hand, even Great-Uncle Sir Eddie was easier to deal with than Eldest-Princess Reyalla. Who was almost certainly the 'certain people' Amanita meant.

Since that was her version of 'discreet,' he couldn't ask directly...

But there was another question he wanted to know the answer to.

"Why do you all call your father's mother 'Eldest-Princess'?" Thony asked them. "She looks Pathremiri, but if she was *your* eldest princess from the last generation, wouldn't she be the queen now? Is she from somewhere el–"

He let his voice trail off because both Amanita and Daffyd were looking rather pained.

"We really should explain," the girl said uncomfortably, looking at her brother. "Before he, like, says something really dumb out in public and it turns into a Big Deal. Because you know Grandmother-Eldest-Princess Reyalla will *make* it a Big Deal."

Daffyd winced and nodded. "*You* explain, sis. *I'm* still eating."

He shoveled in a huge forkful of scrambled eggs as if to make the point.

Or maybe not. Daffyd's eyes were doing little checks on the serving staff who were stationed at the edges of the room, and Thony remembered that the Pathremiri prince had told him that some of the people here were trying to keep Daffyd from growing by shorting him food. Tallness being associated with the Líonar, and therefore to be avoided.

Amanita glared at Daffyd, then sighed. "She's... ugh. There's no good way to say this. Môthir and Vathir are first cousins–"

"*Half* first cousins," Daffyd broke in, with the punctiliousness of someone who is embarrassed and trying to bury the embarrassment in details. "Which is *really* more like *second* cousins."

Amanita shrugged a little. "Yeah, I suppose. And with Puck being our grandfather, I suppose there's no real problems with them being too closely related. We haven't had Snow-Fairies – or Mist-Maidens – in our heritage for thousands of years."

That... didn't really explain anything.

Thony gave them both a blank look. "It's clear I'm missing something. You're not saying your grandmothers are..." He paused as they both winced. "You are. They're sisters."

"*Half* sisters," Amanita clarified. "They had different dads."

Thony frowned. "So... she really *is* or... *was* the 'Eldest-Princess,' then?"

Amanita nodded while Daffyd continued to stuff himself.

"Older than, um, your *other* grandmother?"

Amanita nodded again.

Thony frowned in confusion. "Shouldn't she be Queen then?"

"*She* certainly thinks so," Daffyd remarked dryly as he worked through a pile of sausages. He was going for the denser, more protein-rich foods first, Thony noted.

Amanita sighed. "We do things a little differently here, Thony. The first one of the Queen's daughters to have a daughter herself becomes the Princess-Heir. It's supposed to ensure the line-of-succession for the next two generations."

Thony thought about that. "So... your mom made your grandmother – er, *her* mom – the Heir to the Throne?"

He got another set of nods.

And that made something else click in his head.

"And *you* made *your* mom the Heir? Um, Amanita?" Thony added on a little belatedly as he realized he could have been addressing either of them and should clarify so they knew that he knew what they were talking about.

Amanita nodded again as Daffyd looked up from his food with a sardonic glint in his eye.

Thony frowned. "But your mom is an only child, right? Who else *could* the throne go to, if not her?"

"One of our aunts," Amanita explained. "The daughters of the princesses who didn't get to be queen. We call them '*fal*-princesses' in order to distinguish them from the main line-of-succession."

"What about *you?*" Thony wanted to know. "Your mom doesn't have any sisters, so what happens if *you* don't have some daughters of your own? Eventually."

Daffyd snickered, and Amanita gave him a dirty look.

"The problem doesn't seem to have arisen in the past," the Pathremiri prince explained as his sister shoved eggs and cheese around on her plate, staring hard at it. "There have been a few occasions where a queen had only one daughter, but never for two generations straight. There's no real precedent. Previously, when the Princess-Heir was Named to the succession, her female cousins would lose their titles and become simply 'lady whatever'."

"That didn't happen after I was born," Amanita told her plate. "Instead, Grandmother-Eldest-Princess Reyalla insisted that her daughters – Vathir's sisters retain their titles. And that *their* daughters should be considered for the succession if..."

She bit her lip, but Thony could see where she was going with this.

One of her cousins – a daughter of one of her father's sisters – could take the place she'd been born to if she didn't hop to it and have enough babies to be sure that *one* of them would be a girl. And didn't she say it was the *first* princess to have a daughter who became Heir? It probably wasn't clear if Amanita had to beat her cousins on this...

Given her frequently-expressed opinions on the subject of love and marriage and babies, Thony wondered if...

No, Amanita might hate what she was going to have to do, but she was really attached to her country. She had been raised – and born – to be Queen of Pathremir someday, just like Thony had been born and raised to be King of Aldyrwald. It wasn't something either one of them could easily give up.

"Vathir's sisters are all really nice people, at least," Daffyd said softly, his eyes on his sister. "None of this is *their* idea."

"Not that it matters," Amanita said a little bitterly. "And none of this would be a *Thing* if Môthir and Vathir weren't so closely related. Grandmother-Eldest-Princess Reyalla has made her arguments based on that. She claims that our aunts – *Vathir's* sisters – should be considered *Môthir's* sisters rather than sisters-in-*law*."

Daffyd sighed. "And she's never forgiven our Vathir for being a boy. He's a couple months older, so if he'd been a girl..."

"She'd have been queen," Thony finished for him. He looked at both of them. "Wow. That's... a bit of a mess. How old are your cousins, anyways? *Are* some of them girls?"

Daffyd chuckled, though it sounded a little forced. "That's... actually what makes it even worse from... Grandmother-the-Eldest-Princess' perspective. After our Vathir was born, she had four daughters. And each of *them* has had *only* daughters so far. The oldest one would be Lady Rena of Ilseador – she's almost fourteen."

Thony relaxed a little. "Well, that's good. That gives you some time, I would think."

Daffyd lifted a horizontal hand and tipped it back and forth. "Maybe. Maybe not."

The Pathremiri prince kept his eyes on Amanita as he continued to explain. "The Eldest-Princess hasn't been pushing for Amanita – or any of her other granddaughters – to marry and start trying to have daughters early. She's–"

"She's 'complained' for years about Grandmother-the-Queen having had Môthir at sixteen and *Môthir* having had *Daffyd* at seventeen," Amanita interjected. "She claims that's why neither one of them could manage more than one daughter."

Daffyd nodded. "While you were gone, she was actually campaigning to bring Aunt Fala home from Ilseador," he told Amanita, "even if Rena has to stay there as her father's Heir. Aunt Fala – fal-Princess Falmyra – has four daughters so far," he explained to Thony, "And she might be pregnant again."

He rolled his eyes. "I don't know why they're having so many kids. They surely don't have enough lands to endow each of them. And it's not like here, where a princess has as many daughters as she can in order to maximize her chance of one of them having a daughter if she makes it onto the throne. For that matter – and I love my aunts – I'm not sure why Grandmother-Eldest-Princess Reyalla had four daughters. Once Môthir was born, she knew she didn't have a chance at the throne."

Thony, who was used to seeing families of twelve or thirteen royal children in the Mountain-Region, was less surprised. And he could think of at least one reason why the Eldest-Princess might have thought she'd had a chance to stake her claim.

How many assassination attempts had Daffyd and Amanita's mom – or Amanita, for that matter – managed to survive?

"Davril said something about that," Amanita told her brother. "But Aunt Fala can't come back. She's *Bound* to the land of Ilseador."

Daffyd shrugged. "And there's her three sisters here, so I don't know why it ever really came up, especially if they're willing to leave Rena where she belongs. Alicia is only ten, which isn't older than Aunt Tana's Divya."

Thony felt his eyes starting to cross. Clearly, he needed to go draw up some more charts. "How do you guys keep all of this straight?"

Amanita rolled her eyes at him. "I saw some of those genealogical charts you were putting together to figure out which princesses you could marry back on *your* world, Thony. This isn't really any harder than that."

"Not *mine*," the runaway Crown Prince averred. "Those were *Mama's*. I had just, er, *borrowed* them. To, um, see what she was thinking about."

"And that's why I found you burying them in the freshest pile of stable-sweepings," Amanita snickered half-heartedly.

Thony sighed. "All right, fine. It takes some effort to re-construct those things. I was hoping she wouldn't want to admit to losing them and send to Roger's mother or someone for new ones. Then she'd have to do it all by going back over the Royal Archives to figure out who married who when."

Not that slowing *Mama* down would really have helped anything when it was *Papa* who was arranging a marriage for Thony. And it was less about producing offspring than figuring out how to make a peaceful transfer of power to a neighboring king... and maybe even preventing all-out civil war in the region. *(Stupid name for it. There was nothing* **civil** *about war.)*

"It was one of my less brilliant ideas," Thony conceded.

Amanita gave him a wry grin that lacked most of, well, everything. "So, yeah, that's *our* mess."

And there was really nothing anyone could say to that.

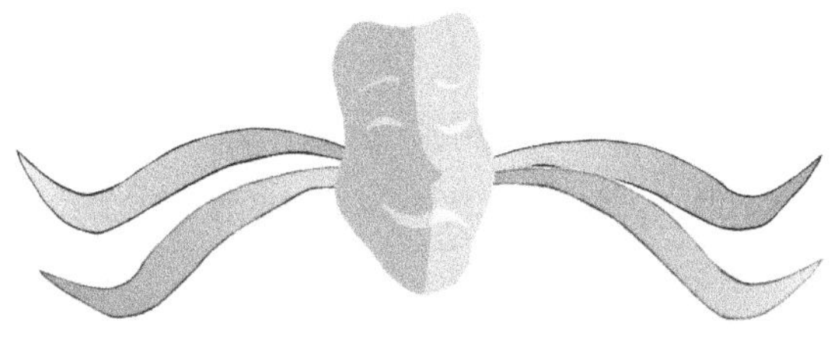

Chapter TWO

An unStable Situation

THE REST OF THE DAY was kind of a mess, too.

And the next few after that.

Puck had stuck around and was being treated as some sort of cross between a foreign dignitary and an ancestor returned from the grave. Which he sort of *was,* Thony gathered, though it wasn't all that clear as to whether he had, um, *fallen for* any previous queens or princesses of Pathremir in the distant past.

He was also not really *acting* like a foreign dignitary or some sort of weird ghost.

The Snow-Fairy Prince/demi-God was spending his time – in between private kissing sessions with the Queen – getting to know his daughter and her husband and trading verbal barbs with the Eldest-Princess. Given that Puck had however-many-centuries of dealing with the various lethal personalities in the Fairy Queen's Court...

...well, suffice it to say that the Eldest-Princess really wasn't *happy*.

And, being the sort of person she was, she took it out on whomever else she could.

Daffyd and Thony took to hiding out from her whenever possible. Amanita was clearly torn, but felt she needed to be learning to stand up to the woman.

It all kind of spoiled her and Daffyd's homecoming, Thony rather thought.

Though it might have been all to the good for people not to be focusing on Amanita's return. As long as everybody's attention was on the resolution of the thirty-three-year mystery of just who Princess Ytheril's father was, they were distracted from starting to figure out what to do with her children.

Or, well, *most* of them were, anyways.

Commander-General Taeryl seemed to find rather a lot of 'reasons' to be in the hallway that Amanita and Daffyd and Thony's suites opened onto. She didn't *say* anything, but her eyes on Daffyd made him cringe and blush.

The Commander-General was an imposing woman close in age to the Eldest-Princess and one of her close cronies. She was tall for a Pathremiri woman – slightly taller than either Daffyd or Thony, even without her towering coiffure and the high-heeled riding boots she wore everywhere.

She was good-looking, Thony supposed, if you were looking at women the age of your grandmother. Her hair was still black *(though she might be dyeing it),* and the various women-warriors around the palace all snapped to perfect attention when she was visible.

"At least none of the others bother you when she's around," Thony consoled his friend as they waited, tucked behind a large pillar, for the coast to clear. "Not like Commander Zaja's troops did on the road."

The rank-and-file members of the all-female troop had all stolen chances to kiss Daffyd while they traveled. He had seemed somewhere between enjoying it and resigned – and he'd never seemed to feel like he could tell them 'no.'

Daffyd sighed. "No one would dare. Honestly, Thony, I'd *rather* be kissing a dozen girls a day than..."

He didn't finish.

Not that he had to.

The *reason* every female from servants to guards to young noblewomen left the Pathremiri prince alone when there was even a *chance* of Commander-General Taeryl being around was that everyone expected an announcement any day that he was betrothed to the older woman.

Everyone... even Daffyd.

Daffyd's valet – a boy just a few years older than his charge, and who also looked after Thony's clothes and suite – had filled them in on what had happened in the Pathremiri prince's absence.

While Daffyd had been out looking for Amanita, Commander-General Taeryl had set aside *both* of her wedded husbands, despite complaints from her grown children. They had been given honorable retirements on some of her farther-flung estates. It was clearly a step taken to obviate objections that a Prince of the Blood could not be taken as a third – and subordinate – spouse.

The whole idea of multiple husbands seemed... weird to Thony.

He'd tried turning it on its head – since the matriarchy seemed to do everything backwards from what he expected and understood. It hadn't helped. While he supposed a rich man – or a king – could *afford* to support multiple wives, it didn't make sense to the runaway prince why he would *want* to. Finding just a *single* princess seemed more than enough work as it was.

Daffyd had looked at him a little condescendingly when Thony had mentioned this.

"She's gone," Thony reported, peeking out again from around the pillar. "And... yup, there go the women she was talking to."

Daffyd put a hand on his shoulder and peeked around as well, to double-check. "All right. Let's go."

They resumed their interrupted journey to the stables.

Twinklestar wasn't in his stall – a loose-box style one where the other side of it opened onto a bit of premium pasture. The two princes went through the unicorn's stall and stepped out into the sunshine.

Thony squinted and shaded his eyes. "I don't see him. Do you want to wait, or shall I call him back?"

Daffyd shrugged. "Waiting is fine by me."

Thony tried not to sigh. The Selavani Court had been more interesting, despite everything being a depressing grey. There had been hunts and gaming afternoons and balls and even afternoon teas.

Here there were some of those things, but it wasn't considered 'appropriate' for boys to join in without a female relative to chaperone them. Daffyd's female relatives were all busy – even Amanita had been sucked into something or other that she refused to talk about – and Thony didn't have any, of course.

So, they were stuck with keeping each other company or seeking out other boys who were similarly unchaperoned. Except none of *those* came to the palace, and apparently Daffyd's friends from before he'd left weren't available anymore. Some had been married off, but others had been warned away from spending time with him after his potentially 'corrupting' time in the outside world.

Presumably Thony sticking to him all the time didn't help with that; Thony was probably considered a corrupting influence all on his own. But Daffyd had said – somewhat absently, when Thony had hesitantly suggested that the older boy didn't *have* to let him follow around all the time if he wanted to hang out with his own friends – that it wasn't that big a deal.

"Have you ever thought of wearing one of those facial-veil-things?" Thony asked as they leaned against the outside of Twinklestar's loose-box on opposite sides of the door. "I saw a bunch of guys wearing them as we rode in from Selavan."

Daffyd sighed, as he always did when Selavan came up in conversation. "No. Not really."

"It seems like that would make it harder for girls to just randomly, um..." Thony wasn't sure how to state it.

"'Take advantage of me'?" Daffyd suggested wryly, his eyes still faraway.

"Er, yeah," Thony agreed uncomfortably.

Daffyd turned his head just enough to give him a lopsided smile before going back to gazing at the distant hedge where the pasture let into a woodsy area. "I don't really mind that part all that much, Thony. I kind of like kissing people."

"Oh." Thony decided to fix his eyes way over there, too. And hopefully he wasn't blushing.

Daffyd had kissed *him* a few weeks ago, shortly after they got to Selavan.

It hadn't *done* anything for him, and Daffyd had never mentioned it or tried again, so Thony had decided to pretend it hadn't happened. After all, the runaway prince didn't have all that many friends that he was willing to lose one just because of a misunderstanding. Or... whatever.

There was a long silence between them, the only sounds being those of stablehands moving around in the rest of the stables at their backs. Thony was very familiar with the sounds in *this* particular stable because he had to come down twice a day to groom Twinklestar.

It was more grooming than the unicorn had gotten regularly in the past, but he liked the attention from his bonded 'unicorn-maiden.' And it was a small burden to take on in return for Twinklestar's offer not to mess his stall – or at least not to complain when 'impure types' cleaned it while he was out. He'd made a whole hell of a ruckus about that latter issue when he'd been in Aldyrwald.

And it also gave Thony – and Daffyd, because the two of them stuck together – an excuse to get out of the stifling atmosphere of the palace for an hour or two. Usually, Daffyd would saddle up his horse and they would all go for a ride together as well. They tried not to mention that to Amanita – *she* didn't seem to be getting any breaks at all from whatever she was working on and it was beginning to tell on her temper.

"Go ahead and ask, Thony," Daffyd said after the silence had stretched out for awhile. "I can almost hear you ready to burst with wanting to."

Ask? Ask what? He had a million questions about all sorts of things, but presumably Daffyd was thinking that *he* was thinking about something related to their last exchange.

"Those friends of yours who aren't coming around," Thony tried. "Did you kiss *them?*"

He glanced over to see Daffyd blink in surprise. "Yes. Some of them anyways."

The older boy gave Thony a curious glance. "That wasn't what I was expecting to hear."

Had he expected Thony to ask him about the kiss in Selavan? *Awkward.*

Thony kind of wondered if the Pathremiri prince had given those other boys more of a chance to say 'no, thank you' than he had Thony. And if not... whether *that* might be part of why they were now staying away. He'd been kind of annoyed at the older boy's presumptuousness, but after watching how the Pathremiri women treated men – including Daffyd – he guessed that it wouldn't even have occurred to Daffyd to ask.

Daffyd was used to being treated as a *thing*. As – what had the Keeterings called it? – a *commodity,* to be bought and sold with no particular intrinsic value of his own. After all, he might be a *prince,* but he was still just a *male,* and therefore interchangeable with any other male. As Commander-General Taeryl's discarding of her other husbands to make space for Daffyd proved. She'd been married to the one guy for thirty years and had two adult sons with him and a daughter, Thony had heard; she'd acquired the other fellow some fifteen years ago and had another daughter that the valet had described as 'probably' being from the second guy.

The whole situation here sucked for a guy, unquestionably. *(Though the valet had whispered to Thony that there were countries out on the 'Merutian Sea' where a man might have multiple wives.*

They called that a 'khareem' and it was considered completely scandalous here in a 'proper Realm like Pathremir.' Thony had forborne to reply that the Pathremiri custom of multiple **husbands** *was pretty darned* **scandalous** *from* **his** *perspective.)*

Thony was uncomfortably aware that in the Mountain-Region back home, there was a certain amount of *interchangeability* in the way princesses were treated. And, he assumed, other women as well.

There were stories of kings – none of the ones nearby, so four or five kingdoms away – who set aside wives of long-standing and even de-legitimized the children of those wives in order to marry a younger princess, or one who was her father's only Heir and therefore her father's kingdom would be her dowry. It wasn't the way the system was supposed to work, at least not the way Thony understood things, and he had no direct evidence of any of it... but he also had no evidence to debunk the stories with either. One of his tutors would have called it 'trying to prove a negative' – you couldn't prove something *hadn't* happened, most of the time.

"What did you think I wanted to know?" Thony asked rather carefully.

Daffyd flashed him a grin. "Whether I liked kissing *you.*"

That led to another silence, as Thony tried to come up with any sort of response that was even mildly appropriate to the circumstances.

"I did, actually," Daffyd said after a moment.

"I see," was the best Thony could come up with.

"I wasn't sure if *you* did, though," Daffyd went on. He still sounded casual and confident – just as he always did when they weren't surrounded by Pathremiri women. But there was just the slightest hint of hesitancy.

Now what in 'all the worlds beyond the Fairy Wood' was Thony supposed to say to *that?*

"Oh," he managed after a moment.

"I kind of left things there, since I didn't know what you thought," Daffyd went on – and really, couldn't he please just *stop* and *drop this?* "Things got kind of busy then. There was so much to *learn* from Inga – I mean, Miss Einirsgeld." There was … something different in his voice when he said the Selavani noblewoman's name. "And... and then we were traveling up here and... I wasn't at all sure about coming back home."

And that was definitely *guilt* in his voice when he said that last.

"Okay," Thony said, since it seemed like some sort of a response was called for.

There were some small noises to his left, and he took the risk of peeking in that direction. Daffyd had turned so he was leaning on his right shoulder, arms folded as he looked at Thony.

"So, what *did* you think?" the Pathremiri prince asked.

There had to be something to say here...

"I thought the divergent views of your history that Miss Einirsgeld and the Keeterings are discovering were fascinating," he said.

Which was absolutely true. And he'd be thrilled to have a conversation about that. Instead of this.

Or about *anything* else, actually.

And there was no real excuse *not* to look at Daffyd if he was going to successfully turn the topic to something less... weird.

Daffyd's eyebrows went up and he looked... almost as if he was briefly tempted to go along with this.

Unfortunately, it was *briefly*.

"Not what I meant, Thony," he said, and his tone was as amused as his face. "Talking about this makes you really uncomfortable, doesn't it?"

Thony rolled his eyes. "Look, Daffyd, we're friends and that's great. Can't we just... leave that other thing in the past?"

Daffyd snickered. "So, is that a 'yes' or a 'no'?"

"You didn't ask a 'yes' or 'no' question," Thony hedged.

"*I* think you liked it," Daffyd declared. "You told us that your country doesn't have hang-ups about this sort of thing, so what's the big deal?"

Thony covered his face with his hands. *"Dude...* Your country *does* have 'hang-ups' about 'this sort of thing,' and your sister is my best friend. So, how could this *not* be a Big Deal? Even if I *were* interested. Which I'm *not.*"

"'Not,' or *'not sure and need to check it out some more'?"*

Daffyd had apparently crossed the distance between them while Thony had his face covered. He was standing... rather close. Invading Thony's personal space again.

Thony winced. *"NOT.* I'm not *interested* in anyone, guy *or* girl. I don't have the *right* to be *interested,"* he began.

"Your Big Quest, yadda, yadda, yadda," Daffyd rolled his eyes. "It's to find someone to marry you, right?"

"A *princess,"* Thony clarified. "Whose *dad* will lend me his *army* to protect Aldyrwald."

"Someone," Daffyd corrected. "And how much of an 'army' do you need anyways? A dozen knights and maybe a couple hundred regular troops? Or the equivalent?"

Thony blinked. He hadn't actually thought about *numbers.*

"About that, I suppose," he admitted, after thinking about it for a moment. "More wouldn't hurt, though."

Papa had a couple dozen sworn knights; they were mostly drawn from their own noble class in Aldyrwald along with a few from four or five countries away who had gotten sick of the wandering life of a knight-errant. And there were several dozen retired knights in the country's three prosperous valleys, though they were mostly old and fat. Papa's five middleborn knighted brothers, and Mama's also might be persuaded to come help.

Which brought the total of knights to... a rather satisfying total.

And if they could count on not being invaded from the direction of Schwannsberg... which seemed somewhat reasonable... There were a limited number of passes through the mountains that could be used to move masses of armed people.

But Papa had no standing army without pulling all the peasants out of the fields. And while those men would undoubtedly answer their king's call to defend their homes, it would likely bring famine to Aldyrwald. No one tried to fight in the Winter, but Spring needed the workers in the fields for planting and lambing and calving and Autumn needed them for harvest and butchering and curing and drying. And pastures and fields of grain and vegetables needed not to be churned to a pulp in Summer or there wouldn't be anything to harvest, even if planting and the rest had gone well.

Which were concerns that the invaders wouldn't have. Actually, if they attacked in the Autumn, they could just raid Aldyrwald's harvest to make up for whatever losses they suffered by making their own commoners serve as soldiers.

So, the neighbors could possibly afford to do this for year after year until Aldyrwald was too worn down with hunger from the ruined harvests to respond. They could even take turns so no one of *them* suffered too much.

(Though that might keep them from invading at all. Thony couldn't quite imagine their greedy, awful neighbors actually colluding effectively like that.)

Of course, *they* would have every knighted *(or unknighted)* youngest son without a settled life-plan flocking to help 'pull down the corrupted Devinthal dynasty.' So, who knew what kind of forces the neighbors could pull together.

Thony had started to get some idea of military logistics while working to the detriment of Valderon Raven'sWing's plans. He'd gotten even more of an idea from... well, from Jost. The street-kid-chieftain had more or less officially apprenticed to Davril Keetering by the time they all split up, and he'd been willing to share what he learned with Thony. During that last week or so when they'd all been living in the mayoral mansion *officially* and by *invitation, (as opposed to when they'd been living surreptitiously in the pickle cellar),* those conversations had tended to happen around the fire in the evenings and the mercenaries had weighed in with their own experiences.

Kamauri and Daennor and Dae were still fairly low-level and had taken more bodyguarding jobs than been part of armies, but Istevan had been serving on campaigns for over ten years and had made officer rank. Had 'just about made it into the strategists' tent before retiring,' was how the older man had put it, with a dry look at his husband. Which seemed to put him pretty high up and meant that he was familiar with every aspect of operations and logistics.

(He'd gotten some ribbing from the younger mercenaries about how that did or didn't fit with the work he was more famous – or infamous – for. Istevan hadn't earned the nickname 'Slyblade' for his campaign-work after all.)

It wasn't likely there was anyone in the Mountain-Region who would know how to manage such large forces.

"You think too much," Daffyd said as Thony ruminated on these new ideas.

And then Thony found himself being kissed without asking. *Again.*

And it was still the same problem. He didn't want to *hurt* Daffyd. He just wanted to be *asked.*

(Well, and for his 'no' to be properly respected.)

And, darnit, but he was starting to understand what Daffyd meant about 'kind of liking to kiss people.' It wasn't *awful,* anyways.

When Daffyd let go of his face, Thony tipped his head down to rest his head on the older boy's shoulder. "Dude. Not cool."

Daffyd snorted. "Don't tell me you didn't like *that.*"

Thony sighed. "I like the *hug* you're giving me now. I'm just not... Look, Jost was *interested,* too. And I told him all the same things. And he suggested that maybe I'm just too *young* to be *interested.*"

"You're not all that much younger than me, Thony," Daffyd sounded skeptical. "You're old enough to *think* you're old enough to go traipsing off onto other worlds."

Thony winced. "Yeah. And that's gone so well so far. I've been here months and the only princess I've come across so far is your sister. Well, I guess and your mom." He felt himself blushing. "Jost said he'd 'try again' when I had to start shaving."

Daffyd's hand gently brushed Thony's cheek. "You mean you haven't been? Hunh. I started when I was thirteen." He sighed. "I suppose this stuff is pale enough that you haven't had to, yet."

Thony's head came up so quickly he nearly cracked Daffyd in the nose. He reached a hand up to touch his own cheek. The older boy was right. There was something there. It was super-soft, though, not like the stiff, curly hairs that were in Papa's beard.

"Well, I'll be," the redheaded young prince murmured, rather distracted by this new idea. "Maybe I should get that shaving kit out that Papa gave me last year."

Daffyd chuckled. "Want me to teach you h–"

He went utterly quiet as an apologetic voice begged 'my ladies' please not to enter the unicorn's stall.

"I suppose there's no point in it anyways," said the distinctive, dismissive voice of the Eldest-Princess. "It's obvious neither the creature nor the boys are here."

The apologetic voice – which Thony was now able to identify as that of the stablemistress – indicated that she hadn't seen either young prince all day. And since Prince Daffyd's horse was still in its stall, likely they hadn't yet come down. The Eldest-Princess dismissed the stablemistress almost rudely, and there was the sound of heeled riding boots moving away.

"You're not going to insist we wait around for them to show up, are you, Taeryl?" Daffyd's unpleasant grandmother said in a gentler – if still exasperated – tone than Thony had yet heard from her.

The Commander-General's voice was determined. "You promised me his hand in marriage when he returned, Reyalla. I've turned my household upside-down for this. I'm tired of waiting."

Thony put his arms around the older boy and tugged them a little farther away from the half-height doors to Twinklestar's loose-box as Daffyd started to shake.

"Taery..." the Eldest-Princess' voice was almost wheedling. "It's just taking a little longer to talk that silly sister of his around. Namarina shouldn't have let her be part of the decision-making process, but there's historical precedent to be satisfied..."

A rough snort. "There's no way you'll ever talk the Queen, the Princess-Heir, *and* that obnoxious child *all* into agreeing." A pause and then the Commander-General's voice went very dry. "After all, you couldn't manage this seventeen years ago either."

"Even a fal-prince's marriage needs to be approved by the Queen..."

"Whatever, Reyalla. I don't know why I listened to you in the first place."

"You listened, darling," the Eldest-Princess' voice turned into a purr, "because it's giving you the unique opportunity to be the mother of a future queen."

Wait, what?

"You make it sound like a done deal, Reya," the Commander-General complained. "There are a lot of things that have to happen before that. *Starting* with me marrying that incredibly handsome grandson of yours."

"I'll make it happen, Taery, stop worrying..." Her voice faded off as they apparently walked out of the stables.

Daffyd was still shaking.

"It's okay," Thony told him. "They're gone now."

"It's *never* going to be okay," Daffyd disagreed. "You heard them. They're going to make me marry her."

They were still sort of hugging, but now Daffyd seemed to be clinging to him rather than... anything else. He tried patting the older boy on the back a little awkwardly. "It sounds like your other grandmother and your mom and Amanita aren't going to let that happen."

"You don't understand," Daffyd's face was buried in Thony's shoulder. "They can't put *Taeryllia Avisdatr* off past a certain point. Not now that I'm fully of age. She's too powerful, since the Army answers to her. The only thing that might work is if there was another offer. But no one in Pathremir would *dare,* not if they're aware that the *Commander-General* wants me. And I doubt there's anyone on the entire plateau who *doesn't* at this point."

Thony snorted. "Dude, if *anyone* understands, it's me. The guy who was going to have to marry an old woman who would try to kill me once the ceremony was over? *And* kill off my dad?"

Daffyd straightened up, looking at him with – oh, no, was that *hope* in his eyes? What had Thony said to suggest... "That's why I was asking about how *many* people you need to defend your land. You saw the troop I had with me to go looking for Amanita. There were fifty women under Commander Zaja. And that's small potatoes for our military. Especially if I could take *men* instead of women. We don't have *knights* the way your people – and some of the surrounding countries here – have, but we have people who do all that same training. *Knights* kind of got a bad name, since it was the Líonar who introduced them to us..."

The dark-skinned boy was kind of babbling, but Thony let him go on rather than arguing.

The whole idea was ridiculous, of course.

"I already asked the Queen," he reminded Daffyd when the other boy finally ran down. "She said 'no'."

"You asked about *armies*," Daffyd said in a pleading tone. "And *knights*. And marrying one of my local cousins. None of the girls would be old enough for years yet – like I told you the other day, Divya's the oldest one in Pathremir and she's only ten. And Rena's only thirteen, even if you were willing to go all the way to Ilseador. And when you say 'armies,' Grandmother-the-Queen is thinking in terms of *thousands* of people. Not a couple hundred rankers who can only be promoted so high."

"Daffyd..." Thony sighed. "I still need an Heir of my own someday."

"You have sisters," Daffyd sounded desperate. "And *they're* married. You told us so. Surely one of *their* children could... oh, wait. Your sisters are Goddesses."

He looked down in frustration and stepped away a little, giving Thony back his personal space at last. "Damn. I forgot about that. Demi-Gods – or, no, their kids wouldn't even be *demi*-Gods, would they. Not with *both* parents being divine. They probably shouldn't rule. It makes things messy, or so history suggests."

Thony was very curious about this 'messy history,' but now was not the time.

He decided not to mention that Prissy's husband, Jeremy, wasn't a God. After all, Jeremy *was* a centaur. The people of Aldyrwald – and the nosy neighbors – might have a thing or two to say about the country being passed to a centaur demi-God.

The redheaded prince ran a hand through his bright mop of curls, his fingers catching in the ponytail he'd been forced to use lately. Nobody here in Pathremir seemed to care that he was a guy and a unicorn-maiden, so maybe he could visit a barber and get it cut. And a shave.

"They said some other stuff, though," he tried distracting Daffyd. "It sounded like they think that Commander Taeryl's daughter – if she's also yours – could be the next queen. But I thought your system doesn't work like that."

That *did* bring Daffyd back from the anxious hand-wringing he'd begun. His gaze sharpened as he frowned over Thony's words, and he started pacing.

"No, it's not. And it *shouldn't*. There's no precedence at all for descent through the male line. Rather the opposite, if anything."

Thony watched the older boy pace and mutter for a minute. "Why wouldn't your grandmother – this one – prefer the crown go to one of her daughters or their daughters? Isn't that what you and Amanita said that's what would happen if... something happened to her and your mom?"

He hated suggesting such things when Daffyd was already so agitated, but apparently this was the right thing to do. Focusing on a problem outside of his own, personal predicament seemed to help the older boy calm down.

"*That's* an easy one," Daffyd said dryly. "Grandmother-the-Eldest-Princess is a terrible mother. She resented my father and my aunts for arriving in the wrong order and never bothered to hide it. They lived out on her country estate while they were growing up and she never brought them to Court or anything except for the requisite

Presentation to the Queen when they were babies. It's how Môthir and Vathir didn't realize they were cousins until they'd already fallen in love and, erm, I was on the way. They'd never met before. Vathir and my aunts all spend most of their time trying to stay out of her way. None of my aunts or my cousins would let the Eldest-Princess be the power behind the throne."

"But *you* would?" Thony was skeptical.

Daffyd waved a hand at that. "I wouldn't be given a say. My grandfather – the Eldest-Princess' husband – had more or less a free hand in raising *his* children because she didn't want anything to do with them. But she's seen how that turned out. And the Commander-General has been close with her since they were girls. Taeryl would do whatever Grandmother-the-Eldest-Princess wanted."

Would she though? The Mountain-Region was fairly stable – now – but there were older stories from before the Peace about military leaders who became a bit too powerful to be controlled. What tools could the Eldest-Princess have to keep the Commander-General in line once the warrior-woman was the mother of a queen-to-be?

Not really Thony's problem... and hopefully not Pathremir's either.

But now Daffyd was back to wringing his hands again. "She'd take my daughter *away* from me. I might not even get to *see* her... I know guys that's happened to..."

For a guy who had seemed – just a few minutes ago – willing to throw it all over for *Thony,* which would presumably make it kind of hard to have kids, he was taking this idea rather hard. On the other hand, Great-great-grandmother Arabella had been raised by her two dads and Istevan and Davril had baby Daphne, so clearly it wasn't *impossible.*

"They also said something about having tried this seventeen years ago and it not working," Thony prodded.

Daffyd blinked and came back alert. *Again.* Good grief, but the guy was either hyperfocused *(on something Thony did **not** want to discuss)* or all over the place *(when there was something Thony **did**).*

"That... they must have been planning for *Vathir* to marry Taeryl." He looked suddenly pleased. "Well, that obviously didn't work. But the timing must have been close. I'll bet that's why Taeryl seems to hate Môthir." He sighed. "She'd only have been about *twice Vathir's* age when he was sixteen. Not more than *three* times. Like with *me.*"

Thony raised his eyebrows. While he supposed he could appreciate the sentiment...

"You never really answered me about those facial-veil things," he pointed out. "You and your dad are both... exceptionally good-looking– Oh, stop that," he interrupted himself irritably as Daffyd's eyes lit with a look of pure mischief. "You know I'm talking about objectively. You have all those servants and warriors and noblewomen trying to kiss you all the time–"

"Stay here long enough and they'll decide *you're* fair game, too," Daffyd told him. "Vathir and I fit the usual aesthetic. You'll be *'exotic'* and *'fascinating'.*"

Thony winced. As he decided to leave as soon as was feasible.

"Be that as it may. It seems like that might... help? Some?"

Daffyd shrugged. "It might keep away the ones that are fun to play with. It wouldn't do a damn bit of good with power-hungry types like Taeryl." He made a face. "And she's likely enough to make me put one on after the marriage anyways. Or even those huge, shapeless robes. Not that any of the guys who have to wear those things think that it stops any of the women from *looking* at them. Rather the reverse, it seems. Some of my friends have told me that they'd feel less naked if they actually *were.*"

Well, *that* was an unnerving thought. Thony had sort of thought all those robes and veils would give a guy a certain anonymity.

He sighed. "At least now we know what Amanita's been working on. And why she's been looking so grouchy."

The Pathremiri prince nodded. "She's a good sister. Even if she really *is* obnoxious."

That was fair.

Brutal, but fair.

"Should we... tell someone about what we heard?" Thony asked Daffyd. "Those seemed like... fairly direct threats to the Queen and her Heirs."

Daffyd looked at him helplessly, drawn back into the current problems. "Who would we tell? I don't doubt that Grandmother-the-Queen is aware of her sister's plans. And probably Môthir as well. Maybe even Amanita."

That was probably true.

It still seemed like they ought to tell *somebody,* though.

"Your dad?" Thony suggested tentatively.

Daffyd shrugged one shoulder. "What Môthir knows, he does. They've never had secrets between them. When she takes the throne, he'll be her co-ruler even if it's not official."

"Well, that really only leaves Puck," Thony noted. "At least of the people *I* know around here."

The older prince gave him a wry look. "If we could ever get him away from Grandmother long enough to talk to him. And I don't know what he could *do* about anything."

"You never know until you ask," Thony said philosophically.

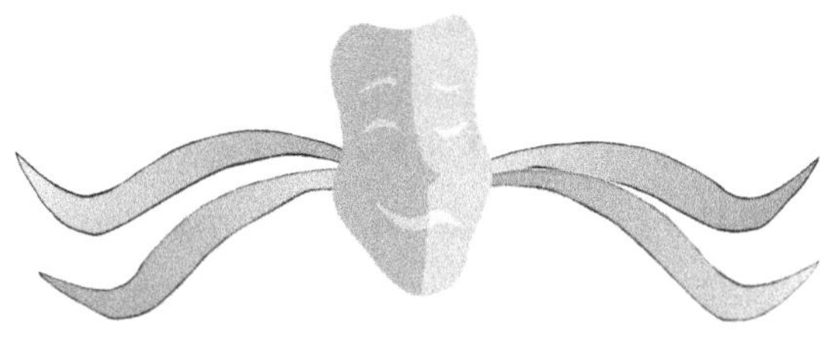

Chapter THREE

A Little Back-Story

TALKING TO PUCK TURNED OUT to be easier than expected.

The next morning, the two boys laid in wait near the entrance to Queen Namarina's rooms and simply waited until she left. And then waited some more while servants came in with breakfast and left again.

It was handy being in a place where no one needed them for anything such that they would be missed somewhere else.

It was also kind of depressing, Thony mused. He... kind of wanted to be needed. Somewhere, but preferably at home. Just... not as a sacrificial bridegroom.

The Prince of the Snow-Fairies was having a leisurely breakfast in bed when they arrived. His shirt was off, and he looked extremely contented.

"Well, if it isn't my favorite prankster and my favorite grandkid!" he greeted the pair as they snuck in and soundlessly closed the door behind them.

"You better not let Amanita hear you saying that," Thony warned. "She's been grumpy enough lately."

Puck gave a small shrug. "I didn't say you were my *only* favorite prankster. I can have more than one." He paused and grinned. "Or I could just call her my favorite grand*daughter.*"

"She's irritated about that, too," Daffyd told him. "You called us your *niece and nephew* when you appeared back in Flowerdust."

"Well, you're that, too, if at a great number of removes," Puck said easily. "My Mother and sisters had... rather a lot to contribute to the Pathremiri lineages back in the days of the Land of Mists. And phrasing it that way let me include Davril and Julanna and Daennor and Dae as well."

He grinned again while Thony and Daffyd looked at each other and thought about who that left *out.* Not that it was likely relevant. Though there *had* been some rather... pointed references to some sea Goddess being interested in what happened to Julanna and Istevan, back when they were all facing off with Shalladra Stillheart.

"What's up?" Puck asked. "Feel free to join me for breakfast," he added dryly as Thony nipped a piece of bacon off his plate.

"We need to talk to you," Thony told him. "And we missed breakfast so we could make sure we caught you alone."

Puck raised an eyebrow and gave Daffyd a be-my-guest gesture at the rest of the food. There really was quite a lot. "You could have just called me, you know. Either one of you."

Thony rolled his eyes. "We didn't want to interrupt while you and the Queen were *busy.*"

Daffyd flushed and looked pointedly out the window.

The Snow-Fairy Prince leaned back on his pile of pillows with a smug expression. "Thoughtful of you. So. What's up? Daffyd?"

"It's Thony's idea," the Pathremiri prince was still focusing on the clouds in the distance. "To talk to you, I mean."

Suddenly Thony realized that Daffyd had actually been *avoiding* Puck.

He gave his friend a worried look, then turned to the Snow-Fairy Prince. "We overheard the Eldest-Princess and the Commander-General talking. They seem to have some sort of plot on to try to take the throne. In the name of the daughter the Commander-General hopes to have, ah..." He ran down, not sure how to finish.

"With me," Daffyd said, his eyes still distant.

"Um, yeah." Thony watched Daffyd watching the sky. "That."

He looked back to see Puck... not-frowning.

"Reyalla and Taeryl have been plotting together since they were children," he said without concern. "Neither Mother nor Silvestria trust them. It's why..."

He paused, then sighed. "Don't tell your grandmother, okay, Daffyd? She thinks it was entirely random chance that we met, way back when. In reality, both Aleri and I were supposed to make sure Namarina had a child before Reyalla – or any of their other sisters."

Daffyd glanced back at the fairy prince in surprise.

Puck looked a bit embarrassed. "Aleri... has a lot of other responsibilities." Not surprising, given that Aleri was the demi-God of Healing, Lies, Politics, and Rogues. "So, it was mostly on me. And I had my work for the Fairy Queen, so it was on and off for me, too.

"When Reyalla finally selected a husband–" and he winced for some reason, "–Aleri happened to be busy. Namarina was still in her wild phase," he smiled reminiscently, while Daffyd looked skeptical, presumably at the idea of his grandmother ever being *wild,* "and she had a great deal more interest in running off to see the world than having a baby to try to claim the throne. She *was* only fifteen after all."

He sighed deeply. "My *plan* was to lure her to a little woodsman's shack up in the mountains where a certain highly self-educated fellow with an excellent background and a caring heart usually spent his Summer afternoons writing philosophical treatises in between chopping wood. *He* could have stayed with her and supported her as her consort...

"Anyways, I got *her* there, but I hadn't actually checked to see if the guy was going to be there that particular day. And he wasn't.

"Not surprisingly, Namarina checked out the shack, found it empty – this fellow didn't leave any of his stuff behind when he wasn't there. No locks, you know. So, she continued on her merry way. I spent the next *two weeks* luring her *back* to that stupid little shack. I even got Eldanor to help me."

Thony's blank expression must have clued Daffyd in.

"He's another demi-God," the Pathremiri prince explained. "Eldanor of the Twisting Trail. Praying to him is supposed to help you when you're lost. Though I thought he was more of a southern continent god," Daffyd directed this to Puck, presumably letting curiosity overwhelm that sense of betrayal. "Isn't it mostly the southern continent *Gajay* who pray to him?"

Puck sipped his tea and gave a one-shouldered shrug. "They're called the *Nuandeleer* over there. And yeah, mostly. But wherever there are roads, Eldanor can be reached."

He seemed to give Thony a particularly pointed look when he said that.

"Anyways," Puck went on, "eventually Namarina caught me. I mean, *literally* caught me. And it's not easy to make a trap that will work for either a fairy or a demi-God. And she told me to lay off on delaying her. And... well..."

He flushed a little and Daffyd and Thony both winced.

Puck chuckled at their reaction. "I wasn't going to tell you anything *inappropriate*. Just... I was very *impressed* with her by then already. And the fact that she *caught* me... well. I didn't *mean* to fall in love with her."

He sighed a little sadly. "When Mother – and my Dear Aunt, the Fairy Queen – found out that your mother was going to be born, Daffyd, I was hoping that they'd give me dispensation to live a mortal's span of years at her side. But there were some things that they felt only I could handle..."

He shook his head. "I was able to come back on and off when Ytheril was very small. Toddlers don't remember things very well, after all, and people don't give a great deal of credence to what they do say. But as she got older – it got complicated. There are... certain biases regarding the children of divine beings. So, no one was supposed to know she was mine."

Thony remembered Daffyd's assertion that things got 'messy' when a demi-God ruled.

Puck nodded, apparently able to see what Thony – what they both? – were thinking. "Exactly. And then, once she was older and could be trusted not to tattle... she was very hurt and angry that she had these vague memories of a father and no one to hang them on. And my love – I mean, Namarina – never married anyone else, so... she never had anyone to take my place."

He looked incredibly torn over that.

Daffyd was starting to look sympathetic.

Thony had remembered something else. "You said – back in the Fairy Queen's Court – that you didn't want to come home yet. Is this... why?"

Puck winced a little. "Yes. After They – the Goddesses – kept me away for so long, I didn't want to come mess things up here. Ytheril had to grow up without a father – without any way to explain why she *looks* so different and *thinks* so differently. It... she's still not really okay with it all."

"Môthir has been crying every night," Daffyd said quietly. "Vathir told us not to worry about it. He's taking care of her."

Puck closed his eyes and his expression went very still. "He's a very good man, Naeel. I... helped out a little bit with them ending up together, too."

"*What?!*" Daffyd seemed more shocked by this than all the rest.

"I came back to check on them – Namarina and Ytheril – when your parents' romance was just starting," Puck told him. "I... tried to do that as often as I could fit it in with my other work, though I didn't let *them* see me. It was all little things. Misdirecting Ytheril's guards so they had more time together. Nudging them so they never actually realized who the other one was."

He gave Daffyd a wry glance. "I don't think I *needed* to do any of it, actually. But... she was my daughter. I wanted her to have the best husband she could find. And that was clearly Naeel. Problematic mother or not."

Thony frowned, trying not to say what he was thinking. Or, given that Puck seemed to be able to read minds, even *think* what he was thinking.

It didn't work, of course. Puck gave him a nod. "Yes, they're a little too closely related. Though half-first-cousins and with such a different heritage as I gave Ytheril... I was still worried. So, I got Aleri to pose as a servant and check her every time she was pregnant, to make sure things went okay."

"*Every* time..." Daffyd whispered, eyes going wide.

Puck's lips tightened. "She's been happier to be with your father than she would have been to birth a dozen daughters, Daffyd. And *he's* been mostly free of that horrendous mother of his."

"A *dozen...?*" Daffyd looked bemused.

Puck rolled his eyes. "I rounded up. By rather a lot. And most of the time it was so early on that she never even noticed that she'd been pregnant. Aleri's very good at what he does." He hesitated. "If it eases your mind any, *he* gave me a lecture when I first asked for his help. With *diagrams*. But after he saw how good Ytheril and Naeel are for each other – and saw Reyalla... Well."

And, Thony guessed, when he saw the look of aching loneliness in Puck's eyes when he talked about his love and his daughter... Aleri had been supremely pissed off at what Valderon Raven'sWing and Shalladra Stillheart – and their unenchanted troops – had done, and had moved around Flowerdust muttering angry Healer things to himself. But Thony had seen the demi-God of Healing's tender heart in a lot of little things – like making sure a lost doll got back to the right little girl, or taking the time to listen to various of the disenchanted people as they cried and talked about the monstrosity of their experiences.

He got a small nod from Puck before that demi-God's attention focused again on Daffyd, who had gone back to staring out the window a while back.

"I've been around for a long, long time, Daffyd," Puck said softly. "And these last thirty-some years have been the absolute hardest I've ever lived through. Missing out on most of Ytheril's life. Missing out on you and your sister. Being here with my true love... for the few years we might have together..."

Daffyd looked over and met Puck's eyes. His expression was still... hurt. "But you were going to keep staying away, you said. And... when we came home last week, you disappeared. You listened to me worrying about what was going to happen when we got home, and... you *left* me." He paused. "And you weren't planning to come back, were you?"

Puck looked down first.

"I don't own my own time, Daffyd. I never have. I left – so long ago – and never let Namarina or Ytheril see me thereafter because... they – and you – were going to age. And I... won't. I haven't. You saw how Namarina felt self-conscious about how she appeared after you summoned me. Someday... someday she'll be *old,* Daffyd. And someday thereafter, Ytheril will. And then you. And your sister. And I'll... still look about the same as I do now.

"After such a long gap... after not being here when she – when all of you – needed me... I didn't think you'd want..." He stopped suddenly and swallowed hard. His hands clenched the sheets and blankets covering his lower half.

"No. That's not true. *I* wasn't given the choice. My Mother... the Fairy Queen – the Great Goddess, rather – I think *They* would have let me stay. It was Silvestria who decided that Her Line of Pathremiri Queens must be left undisturbed by my presence more than I'd already done. And it's Silvestria who's still preeminent here."

Daffyd looked confused. "But..."

Thony waved a hand. "Excuse me. I know I've heard that name before, but just who is this Silvestria-person again?"

Puck gave him a sad, wry look. "That would be *Who*, not *who*, Thony. Silvestria is the Silver Dragon Goddess of Pathremir and Dawil, the Lady of Wild Places, the Goddess of Gentle Darkness. Or, as they're now calling Her in Selavan, the Goddess of Light and Dark."

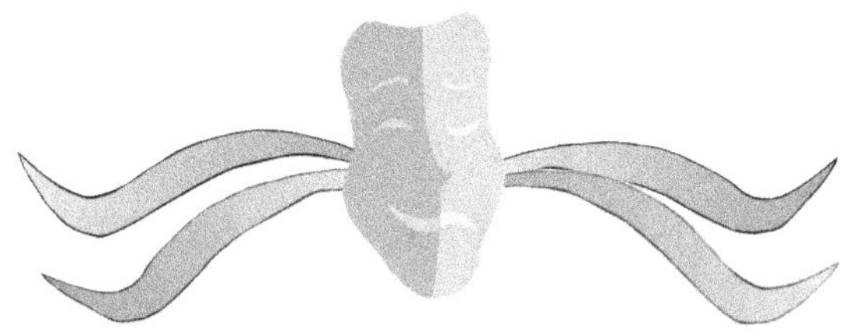

Chapter FOUR

Dealing with Dragon Ladies

"Isn't She going to be a little annoyed that you're here *now*, then?" Thony asked. "Or that you've told us all this stuff?"

The Snow-Fairy Prince shrugged. "She and my Mother are arguing about it. Mother says that since I'm no longer the Puck – just another of Her Sons and not a particularly important one at that – Silvestria should just back off and leave things alone."

Thony gave him a thoughtful look. "I don't imagine telling a *dragon* to back off works all that well."

"She's... not a Dragon all of the time," Daffyd commented a bit weakly.

"*Enough* of the time," Puck – or rather Prince Skiftglow – muttered.

"So... you might *stay?*" Daffyd asked hopefully.

Skiftglow winced. "I'd like to. But it depends on what agreement the Ladies come up with."

"If it helps," Thony volunteered, "You could pass on the word that at least *some* of the 'Pathremiri Line of Queens' are already rather, um, *royally pissed off* with regards to Goddesses. Amanita, anyways," he explained as Daffyd gave him a shocked look. "She seems to take it as a personal insult that the original inhabitants of the Land of Mists didn't get help from, well, *either* Goddess for some thousand years after the Líonar appeared."

"Amanita takes *everything* as a *personal insult*," Daffyd muttered, but he was looking out the window again. Thony suspected Daffyd pretty much agreed with Amanita.

Or at least he did *now*.

"I'm just saying," Thony put on an innocent look. "Taking you away again won't help. And if the queen of a land refuses to honor the Gods... that probably doesn't look good when They have... God-get-togethers or whatever. Though, granted, that's probably a good long ways off, since her mom and grandmother both seem healthy."

Prince Skiftglow gave him an amused look. "God-get-togethers... Not what They call it, but you make a good point."

He looked thoughtfully at the pair of boys. "You know... that point might be made just a *tad* more forcefully if *you* told Them yourselves."

Daffyd's head swung back in shock, but Thony just sighed. Puck had mentioned back in Flowerdust that Thony was to travel to Pathremir with them because Puck's Mother wanted to meet Thony. So, the redheaded prince had sort of been anticipating having to make some kind of excursion to do that. Eventually.

"You mean right *now?*" he asked.

Prince Skiftglow shrugged. "I'm not a put-it-off kind of guy myself. But it's up to you, really. The *both* of you." He looked hard at Thony, flickering his eyes at Daffyd and back.

Well, that was just peachy.

Thony had just about decided that he was going to move on soon anyways. It was high Summer right now, which was a pleasant time to be up here in the mountains. But if he wanted to go somewhere, waiting till the beginning of Autumn – or worse, the first snowfalls – was not a good plan. Mama and Papa hadn't let him travel around the Mountain-Region, Winter *or* Summer, but he'd listened to the tales of those who did.

And... it really wasn't the business of Queen Namarina or any of her people – or even Amanita – just where Thony went and what he did. They'd been kind, and he'd hope to repay their kindness, but he had a mission and – aside from Daffyd's crazy idea – there was no way he was going to fulfill it here.

He *had* to go on.

On the other hand, *they* probably weren't likely to agree with that assessment, so he'd planned to, ah, *leave discreetly* when he was ready to go. He had some experience with that already, after all.

Taking Daffyd along would be an entirely different story.

First of all, Daffyd's whereabouts really *were* the business of, well, *everyone in Pathremir.*

Secondly, they had a *lot* more people to send looking for Daffyd than Papa did for Thony.

Thirdly, there *was* Daffyd's crazy idea, which would make travel together... *awkward.* Particularly considering that Thony was looking for a bride.

*(Although he kind of had the idea that propositioning – or proposing or whatever – **him** had really been more of a last-ditch act of desperation for Daffyd.)*

Fourthly, there was *no way* this wouldn't be viewed as Thony kidnapping the Pathremiri prince. Daffyd was *way* too much of a rules-follower to think up something like this on his own. Even getting him to agree to sneak in here with Thony to talk to Puck had required pointing out that there wasn't *actually* a rule against doing it. *(Though that might have been as much about Daffyd not wanting to talk to Puck as anything else.)*

Fifthly, traveling with a total rules-follower like Daffyd might be a pain in and of itself. For just one example, their party had stayed at inns *(where Commander Zaja had locked them up every night and stationed guards everywhere)* on the entire trip back from Flowerdust, except when they'd stayed in someone's house or castle. Whether Daffyd would even *agree* to sleep on the ground was still entirely up in the air from Thony's perspective.

And finally... Amanita was going to be absolutely *livid* that Thony had taken *Daffyd* instead of *her*.

Though she wouldn't be *with* them to do any complaining...

Daffyd's reaction was a bit less blasé.

The Pathremiri prince went pale – which, with that dark brown skin of his made him look kind of ashy.

"*Me?*" he blurted. "Meet the *Goddesses?*"

Skiftglow gave him a sympathetic look. "They're both your Grandmothers, Daffyd. At one number of removes or another."

Daffyd did not look reassured. Presumably his experience with 'grandmothers' to-date hadn't really prepared him to see that as a point of comfort. "You'll come with us, right?"

Thony rolled his eyes as Skiftglow shook his head regretfully. Or maybe that was *'fake regretfully.'* "Not a good idea, Daffyd. Possession is always nine-tenths of the law. If I leave here, it's that much easier for Them to keep me from coming back."

He leaned back in his bed again and put his hands behind his head, elbows out. "You and Thony will be fine. He's met a few Gods and Goddesses already, haven't you?" He switched to addressing Thony halfway through, and Thony had to allow as that he had.

Prissy and Joanna counted, right? And that terrifying Fire Goddess Cythera – Who, honestly, had probably been just as terrifying before She was a Goddess. She just had that kind of personality.

And Lilysong, the Fairy Queen. Who was so much more than just queen of the fairies.

And then Roger and Phillip and Aleri and Puck – no, *Prince Skiftglow* – himself.

And maybe Lady Opalsinger and Lord Aspenheart. Didn't Amanita – and Stillheart – say that a prince or princess of their kind of elves was basically a demi-God?

It wasn't something Thony wanted to do every day, and intentionally seeking out Deities rather than running across them by accident wasn't really his Thing, but...

Daffyd was regarding him *very* dubiously.

"A Quest is good for the soul, grandson," Prince Skiftglow said, his phrasing making it sound like a directive from an older relative, instead of a pretty insane idea from a friend. "Every young person should complete one before going on to other things. Come back in an hour and I'll have directions for you to reach my Mother's palace."

He shooed them out of the room.

They went out into the queen's sitting room, Thony closing the door carefully behind them. He turned around to see Daffyd standing, hip-shot, with a very bemused expression.

"So, what are we supposed to do now?" the older boy asked.

Thony shrugged. "Get ready to go, I imagine. Do you still have your saddlebags?"

"They're down in the stables with my horse." Daffyd answered automatically. "Wait, you mean you want to go *today?* Like, right *now?*"

"Well, in an hour or so," Thony agreed. "He told us to come back to get a map. Or directions or something."

Daffyd looked at him blankly. "But that's impossible. It takes *days* to arrange an expedition like this. Just talking to Grandmother-the-Queen, Môthir, Vathir... Let alone rearranging troop assignments – most of the women expect to go home every night, or at least on their break days, and–"

Thony cast what he hoped was a veiled look of disgust at the closed bedchamber door. "Daffyd. Dude. We aren't *telling* people that we're leaving. We're just going to get our stuff together and *do* it."

He was already running through ideas in his head for how to make that happen.

Daffyd's mouth was hanging open in shock.

Oh, yeah, traveling with this guy was going to be *great*.

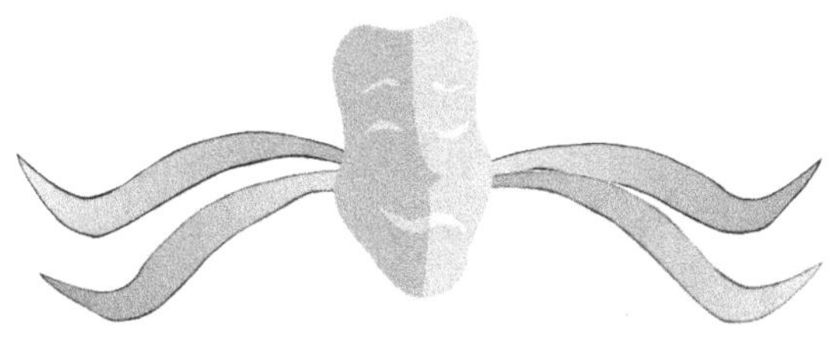

Chapter FIVE

Here We Go Again...

ONCE DAFFYD GOT HIS HEAD wrapped around the idea, things went more smoothly.

It was more like two hours before they met Prince Skiftglow again. Daffyd had insisted on writing letters to practically everyone in his family to apologize for their departure. When he started dithering on about letters to his aunts, Thony wrastled the pen and paper away from him.

They left the letters tucked under his pillows where a not-too-difficult search would find them. Hopefully the next day.

Daffyd had also argued *(but ultimately yielded)* to the need for re-directing the search. Thony had suggested he imply that they were heading back to Selavan, and that it had something to do with his threatened nuptials to Commander-General Taeryllia Avisdatr.

Since – as Daffyd himself had pointed out yesterday – the only way to completely avoid those nuptials was to find a different bride, that should get absolutely *everybody* riled up, if for a variety of different reasons. Daffyd's own flush more or less convinced Thony that there was enough truth to the implication to make it entirely plausible. And likely he'd need to find a way to help Daffyd get back to Selavan before they were done.

And then there had been the matter of whittling Daffyd's traveling supplies down to essentials and figuring out how to get those essentials out to the horses.

They were taking Daffyd's mount – a rather showy black horse that Thony was dubious would handle off-roading terribly well, Silverfoot, and Twinklestar. The unicorn was very pleased to be getting out and about again, though he admitted he'd enjoyed the respite. He was also perfectly willing to lead Silverfoot and Nightbreeze out of the city.

Prince Skiftglow had an answer to the problem of getting their supplies down to the stables, the horses released, and the tack and saddles and saddlebags all properly attached so nothing important was lost. He offered to deal with it himself.

Since Skiftglow/Puck had pretty much ditched him and Amanita in the *middle of a war-zone* and left them to fend for themselves, Thony had no compunctions about taking the Snow-Fairy Prince *(who might not be the Puck anymore, but was still the demi-God of Pranks and Mischief and had who-knew-what mad powers to accomplish it all with)* up on his offer.

Daffyd looked more dubious and guilty.

Of course, '*dubious and guilty*' had become Daffyd's default expression. Hopefully it would clear up once they got out of the city.

He'd been dubious-and-guilty while they snuck down to the palace kitchens and obtained traveling food.

He'd been dubious-and-guilty when they snuck into the palace laundry to obtain robes from the stash of such things kept for general use.

And he'd been – by God! – dubious-and-guilty when Thony had them search his room for all the coins they could find to take with them. His *own coins,* leftover from spending money he'd been given over the years!

Prince Skiftglow, however, approved of their plans and told them where to get started. He had written instructions for them as well. He handed those to Thony after seeing Daffyd displaying about three different and simultaneous nervous tics.

And he told them to stick together.

And fed them a good solid lunch.

At least the food seemed to calm Daffyd down. A *little.*

So, some *three* hours after they started getting ready, a pair of very modest guys in full robes and veils made their way out of the city. They stayed on main roads and away from alleyways.

And they ignored the women and girls who shouted encouragingly to them in the wealthier districts or provided rude and curious commentary in the poorer ones.

Once, a patrol of City Guardswomen stopped them. The five women *(and they didn't look a great deal older than Thony, so he was being generous)* surrounded them and came *far* too close for comfort.

Daffyd completely froze, but they had discussed something like this happening and he ended up answering the questions put to them *('where are the women who should be chaperoning you?' segued into 'just what do you have on underneath there?'... which was beyond uncomfortable even just listening and was surely well beyond what was reasonable).*

After all, if Thony spoke up, they'd be able to tell right away that his accent was all wrong.

"You did fine, dude," Thony said reassuringly as they continued on their way after that incident.

He glanced back over his shoulder. "About the only thing they could tell for sure was that you're upper-class."

After having been shouted at for the last couple hours, Thony could tell the difference between the accents from the richer and poorer parts of the city.

"This is *insane,*" Daffyd hissed back. "We should report those Guards. I'm going back. Now."

Thony sighed. "Fine. Sure. You can do that. Your grandfather will probably help you sneak back in before you're even missed and no one will ever know."

Daffyd's eyes were impossible to see behind the layer of fabric, but Thony guessed he was getting a suspicious look. "You're not going to try to tell me not to?"

Thony shrugged. "I can't *make* you do anything. Twinklestar can probably get your horse back to where Prince Skiftglow can pick it up."

Daffyd's well-disguised body posture changed. Slumping, Thony suspected, though without a facial expression it was hard to tell if it was in relief or disappointment. And then he seemed to tense up again.

"What about you?"

"I have the directions on how to get to where we're going, so I should be able to handle it," Thony said nonchalantly. "Give my best to Amanita. And to your wife. I don't think I'll be coming back this way before you get hitched."

Daffyd went frozen again, which got them some nasty remarks from other passersby until Thony managed to tug him back into the flow of traffic, muttering about how he could come with or go back, but standing still in the middle of a busy street was *not* a thing.

"You've got me coming and going, don't you, Thony." It wasn't really a question and Daffyd's tone was kind of bitter.

"Hmmn?" Thony had only learned to negotiate intersections a few months ago and Flowerdust was never this busy. Dynsfyor and Dysacha had been *way* busier, but he hadn't been let free to move around on his own. This was the first time he'd had to do this sort of thing independently and it took a certain amount of concentration.

"If I go back," Daffyd went on, "then I'm stuck all over again. This might be my chance to make choices for myself. But..."

"But that means you actually have to make choices. For yourself." Thony tried to make his tone sympathetic instead of exasperated. It wasn't like taking the Pathremiri Prince along had been *his* idea, after all.

Though Daffyd's presence on this trek through the city had been valuable. When he'd decided to snag the robes and veils, Thony hadn't fully appreciated that guys didn't move around as individuals.

Or rather, a number of guys *did,* but they were clearly in an, um, *different echelon* of society. Guys who bothered to put on robes and veils – or whose womenfolk required them to do so – were viewed as *'must be something special,'* and all the passersby wanted to see just why.

Kind of a mess, since it garnered them more attention as they moved farther from the palace and the city center. Thony guessed guys in robes and veils didn't come down this way super often. They wouldn't soon be forgotten – though the folks on these streets looked about as willing to share info with authorities as Jost's street-kids.

On the other hand, no one could tell exactly *who* they were, which was probably even more critical. Even if – as Thony suspected, given by how nervous his friend was – Daffyd hadn't been allowed out in public often enough to be recognized for himself, he looked a great deal like his dad, and the Prince-Consort had been in the public eye for seventeen years.

Not to mention that, compared to a lot of the folks on the streets, Daffyd really *was* extremely good-looking.

And that wasn't even beginning to deal with how totally *not* inconspicuous Thony's bright red hair and pale skin would be in this city – this *nation* – full of brown-skinned, black-haired people.

"You haven't been out on your own a lot, have you?" Thony noted as Daffyd shied away from a group of women who came close enough to tug on their robes and make some off-color jokes as they passed. Not that he wasn't uncomfortable with that himself, but his weeks in Flowerdust around the street-kids had apparently inured him some to this kind of behavior.

The villages around Castle Devinthal, Thony had begun to realize were inhabited by people more on the level of what was considered 'middle-class' elsewhere. In their behavior, anyways.

His own family's 'luxurious' castle had only been about as fancy as Flowerdust's mayoral mansion; it hadn't measured up to any of the other, fancier places he'd been here. *(Although the Keetering sisters had called the inn in Dysacha – and the Court – 'tasteless.' And the king's castle in Selavan had been weirdly dark and depressing despite the many energetic activities that all the resident nobility involved themselves in.)*

Daffyd shook his head – or at least his robes moved slightly. "Not at all in the city. Vathir used to take us camping in the hills and forests behind the palace when we were small... We knew there were Guards watching over us, even if we couldn't see them. It was just fun to pretend that we were all alone."

Thony gave the pile of clothing that contained his friend a sympathetic look. "That was pretty much what it was like for me, too. I could move around anywhere inside the castle compound... but they only started letting me go down to the nearer village last year. And to take short rides into the forest a few months ago."

He sighed. "And by 'forest' I mean the little copse of trees between the near village and the far village in the biggest of our three valleys. I don't know if there's a thousand people in both of them put together. And we live in the mountains... but the first time I'd ever been on mountain slopes was when we rode up here from Selavan."

Daffyd was silent for a few minutes after that, and Thony began to wonder if he'd laid it on too thick. It was all *true*... and he'd felt incredibly smothered when he was at home. But after seeing how circumscribed Daffyd's life was, he was aware of how much freedom of movement he actually *had* possessed.

They'd made it onto some *super*-grungy streets before Daffyd finally spoke again.

"So... how'd you get so easy about all this, then?"

"Sheer terror," Thony answered casually. "I mean, I'd always *wanted* to go on a Quest – even if it had to be to rescue a princess, it seems like it would have been fun." He paused. "And I didn't want to end up one of those princes who has to be rescued by a Worthy Miller's Daughter. I mean, they're always beautiful, kind, and wise, but that's just so super embarrassing, you know?"

A sound like a muffled snort from under Daffyd's layers, and his voice was kind of wistful. "I wouldn't mind being rescued by a beautiful girl."

Cultural differences, Thony reminded himself.

"Well, anyways," the redheaded prince went on after a moment, "Once I realized I wasn't going to get to go on my Quest – or even get rescued by a WMD – the only options were stick around to be married off to some old middleborn princess who'd be under orders to off me and Papa so that Aldyrwald could belong to her brother or nephew or... whatever," grand-nephew... "or run away and try to find a way to solve the problem with outside resources."

(I.e., find that princess-bride with the powerful father to lend him armies.)

(Or a 'relatively' small number of knights and men-at-arms.)

(Which reminded Thony of Daffyd's crazy idea...)

(Sigh.)

"What does 'middleborn' princess mean?" Daffyd asked. "The way you say it makes it sound more important than just the words suggest."

"Hmmn?" Thony was keeping a discreet side-eye on a bunch of raggedy street-kids who had been pacing them for the last three blocks. "Oh, yeah, Amanita thought it was weird, too, for some reason. In the Mountain-Region we're all careful to have kids in lucky numbers – you know, three, seven, or twelve, though onlies are okay. The oldest inherits if they're a boy, of course. Or if they're a girl and there are no boys. And the oldest and youngest princesses get arranged-rescue-marriages. The youngest prince can usually arrange for a princess-heir to rescue. The middleborns go off to become itinerant knights-errant if they're boys, or maiden-aunts if they're girls. Sometimes the middleborn knights-errant come back home or settle down somewhere else when they get old, though they seem to find that shameful. One of Papa's great-uncles lives with us, but Papa's middleborn brothers have flat-out refused to."

He sighed. "I'm *hoping* that I can get them to come back – and maybe Mama's as well – for long enough to put on a show of force and family solidarity when I get back home."

That froze Daffyd's feet again, and Thony urged him on a little uneasily. The street-kids he'd been watching seemed to have disappeared... but if he understood how these things worked, that probably just meant they'd crossed over into someone else's territory.

"So..." Daffyd seemed to be having trouble with the idea. "Just *how* many people does that add up to?"

Thony shrugged absently. "It's hard to get up to twelve – or even seven – kids of the same gender. Most families stop with three of a kind. Mama is the youngest of three girls. Papa is the oldest of seven boys. Oh, Mama has seven older brothers, too. *Her* youngest brother never found a princess though, since Mama never finished making his nettle-shirt to turn him back from being a swan – Uncle Tommy's right arm is still a wing, and his parents couldn't find anyone willing to let him rescue their daughter and rule their land, even if he could manage to do it. There's always some like that, so the numbers work out about right in the end."

He decided not to discuss the rather dark ideas he'd occasionally entertained regarding just how the royal families managed to end up with such perfect, gender-balanced sets of lucky-numbered children.

"You're joking," Daffyd said. His tone was shocked, but at least his feet kept moving. "You can't seriously tell me that you have *eleven* aunts and uncles who don't have a prayer of ever having homes or families of their own? Do the lesser nobles and common people act this crazy as well?"

Thony shot the fabric-swathed blob that was Daffyd an uneasy glance. "I don't know. The millers at least seem to shoot for lucky numbers of kids. And some of the nobles, maybe. Peasant families seem to have lots of kids."

He hesitated as Daffyd's silence started to seem... *judgy*.

"Look, Daffyd, none of this is my idea. It's just the way things are at home. *I* would have been up for marrying Princess Sophia from Schwannsberg – the next kingdom over. She's my brother-in-law Roger's middleborn sister and she's nearly twenty. And Roger's a middleborn and he's a great guy."

"So why didn't you?" Daffyd asked. "Marry this girl?"

Thony sighed. "Because *her* father – who used to be Papa's best friend since they were kids – told Papa that he'd have to be dead before another one of his children married one of Papa's. Joanna and Roger got married when they were on *their* Quest and King Richie didn't really have a chance to forbid it."

He paused. "Sophia's not a particularly bad sort, even if she *is* a middleborn. At least she's closer to my own age than the creaking old ladies that the *other* neighbors were willing to offer for me. After all," he added a little bitterly, "if they gave me one of their *daughters*, instead of their own aunts, one of those girls might be desperate enough to disobey her father's instructions to off me."

Another moment of silence went by.

They were starting to pass out of the grungy city streets. The road they were on was starting to look like it was turning into more of a country lane. Thony started to relax a bit.

"What a waste," he thought he heard Daffyd mutter, and decided to ignore it.

"What's a nice pair o' laddies doin' out this end o' town?" A tough-looking girl had stepped out in front of them. Thony didn't have to look around to know that they were surrounded. He'd been through this before, after all, and then he'd hung out enough with Jost's crew to understand that street-kids worked like a pack of feral dogs. And for the same reason: survival.

"Our Môthir's estate is out in the country, but she's bad with numbers," Daffyd repeated the excuse they'd both come up with before. "She sent us in to town to see the tailors, but she forgot to give us enough to pay for a carriage back."

Thony tugged on Daffyd's robed arm, trying not to make it look urgent.

"Oh, yeah," Daffyd added, not very convincingly. "My brother hates it when I say things like that about her. *He* thinks she didn't realize that the tailors would make us pay for the clothes she wanted made before they would cut the cloth. They took every last copper we had."

He tried to sound mournful and irritated... and came off sounding terrified.

"Tradesmen are the worst," said a tall boy, coming up to stand behind the girl. "Cain't trust 'em worth a damn, eh, Rissa?"

The girl glowered up at him for an instant, then looked back at Thony and Daffyd with narrowed eyes. "Ye mus' think I'm a fool t'believe that fellows rich enough to afford all them clothes haven't pouches o' coin hidden under all them layers?"

That was a fair complaint.

Especially since they *did,* indeed, have pouches of coins under their robes. Thony had made sure the pouches were tucked right against their skin, underneath both shirts and tunics so they couldn't be taken by pickpockets, and bound tight so they wouldn't jingle *(and a thank-you to Skylir for teaching him that trick... the hard way).* They'd have to be literally stripped to the skin to be robbed.

Not that these kids looked like they would mind doing that.

But Jost had told him to always make sure there was *something* to give up in an emergency.

"We... we have a little left," Thony said softly, trying to imitate Daffyd's accent. "Please... if our mother doesn't get back the change she expects, she'll beat us."

The tough girl – Rissa – folded her arms and rested her weight on one leg while she gave them a skeptical look. "On'y reason a country-lady'd send 'er boys fer clothes in th'city is a-cause she's gettin' ready to wed them off. Ain't gonna damage th'goods afore she makes the sale, now is she?"

Damn. Thony hadn't thought of that.

"She'll... she'll beat us where it won't show," Daffyd volunteered. At least now that anxious voice worked. "This is so she can show us off to potential brides. There'll be time for us to heal up after that and before... before the weddings.

"Please," he suddenly begged, sounding entirely sincere. "If she gets carried away and makes us ugly, we'll end up as third husbands to nasty old women. My brother's already no treat – he needs all the help he can get."

The tall boy looked sympathetic, but the girl didn't.

"So?" she demanded callously. "What's it to us?"

"Just let me give her what we have," Thony pleaded.

"Fine." Daffyd made a gesture that was... a little too royal in Thony's opinion.

But it freed the younger boy to unhitch his decoy purse from his belt and dangle it out of his drooping sleeve for the girl to take. He made sure not to let his overly-pale-for-a-Pathremiri fingers show beyond the shadow of his sleeve as he did so.

Rissa poured the coins – all copper – out into her hand and counted them. Her lip curled in disgust and she glared up at Thony, who stepped behind the slightly taller Daffyd as if seeking protection. In reality, Daffyd would be pretty useless if they had to fend these kids off – he was even worse than Thony with a sword. Not that they had swords with them, since those couldn't have been concealed beneath their robes. Puck – Prince Skiftglow – had promised to teach them both some barehanded self-defense, but he hadn't gotten around to it.

"Not 'ardly worth it," she commented to someone standing to the side. Thony didn't turn to look, and neither did Daffyd, so apparently, he also knew that you don't take your eye off the alpha dog in the pack. "Mebbe we should see what else they 'ave 'idden."

"*That* ain't worth it," said a higher, sweeter voice from their left and rear. "Takes it from robbery to *assault*. An' *assault* on men in full robes get tracked down. People like their mama *know* people."

Rissa pouted at that, and Thony revised his opinion of who was in charge here. From his position slightly behind the trembling Daffyd he dared a peek to find the speaker.

Was she the tiny girl with the devilish expression or the sloe-eyed one who was taller than Daffyd and slender as a willow?

"Mebbe they don't get to report neither," the tall boy behind Rissa suggested, and she reached backwards to slap him across his face without even looking. Thony switched back to watching him nervously. Correction or not, the tall boy was cracking his knuckles ominously and giving them a rather smug look despite the red mark across his mouth from Rissa's slap.

"I know we don' keep ye 'round fer yer wits, Blue, but tha's dumb e'en fer *you*," commented the person behind. "Ye all heerd the firs' one. Sounds like they ain't just *rich*, they've *class*. Lads like this don' go *missin'*."

"Th'second one didn' sound like *class*," someone off to their right. "Actually... 'e didn't sound quite right at all."

Daffyd reached around and put an arm around Thony's shoulders, pulling him close like a protective older brother might. "My little brother's had a speech impediment since he was a lad. I told you he wasn't a treat on the marriage market. That's part of it."

"He's not... but *you* are, I take it?" commented Rissa with a look of... was that avarice or lust? It hardly mattered. From Thony's perspective the emotions were the same, with the only difference being the object of the greed.

"Not really," Daffyd said. "Hopefully enough so I don't get stuck with an old woman is all I hope." He paused. "Which will also happen if you compromise our modesty. It's bad enough if anyone finds out we had to walk home like this."

Rissa snorted. "What's that t' us?" she said again, looking over Daffyd's shoulder at her boss. "If we cain't check 'em out all proper fer more coin–" and she didn't add the words *'because you're too cowardly,'* but they hung in the air, and Thony guessed there would be a battle for dominance of this gang sometime soon, "–then how's aboot we take a peek at what man-meat with *class* looks like up close, aye?'

There was a brief staring contest, but after Rissa lowered her eyes the person with the high sweet voice agreed that there wasn't much harm in *that*. Getting a peek at the good-looking one anyways. Not much point in bothering with the one who 'wasn't a treat' in his own brother's words.

Thony felt hands on his arms and he was pulled away from Daffyd's side by hands that didn't try to lift his robes but were getting decidedly too *familiar* through the insulating layers of cloth.

And he had to watch as the tall, slender girl roughly jerked Daffyd's hood back and Rissa ripped the veil from his face. Daffyd stood there, barefaced and flushed, but he lifted his chin a tad and looked down his long, straight nose at them all.

There was a bit of a silence as the folks at the back circled around to get their own peek. It might have made a good chance for the Pathremiri prince to make a break for it, given that they were... *mightily* distracted... if he'd been willing to leave Thony behind.

The redheaded boy wasn't actually sure if he hoped Daffyd would try. If the older prince could get away fast enough to summon help... that *might* be a good thing. But chances were, these kids were fleeter of foot than Daffyd, and with all those flapping robes they'd have a great deal to grab for. Likely he wouldn't even make it out of their circle.

"Well, well, well," that high, sweet voice belonged – weirdly enough – not to either of the girls Thony had guessed, but to a person whose bulky, muscled, but obviously-underfed form suggested a male. "Ye look a rather great deal like the Prince-Consort, lad."

Daffyd pursed his lips and said nothing.

The guy with the high voice tilted... *their* head, then commented over their shoulder to Rissa. "I think we've been fed a pile o' horseshit. This ain't a coupla lads tryin' t'git home. 'Tis our good Prince Daffyd runnin' off with 'is *boyfriend.*" Thony got a condescending look, then the focus returned to Daffyd. "Am I right, *Yer Highness?*"

Daffyd clearly weighed trying to bluff it through, then sighed and shook his head. "Not quite. That's just my servant. When I decided to run off, he insisted on coming with me."

Rissa snickered, though her eyes were still round as she stared at Daffyd. Apparently, he was even more good-looking to a Pathremiri girl than Thony had realized. "Not a boyfriend *yet,* then. Cain't imagine it'll stay that way once'n he has ye alone."

Thony rolled his eyes. Good grief. Couldn't guys just be *friends?* Or *loyal* to each other?

The Pathremiri prince folded his arms and said, "I don't lean that way," in an offended tone.

Which made Thony roll his eyes *again.*

There was something to be said for these veils. You didn't have to worry about betraying your thoughts and could make whatever faces you liked.

"Seems like there'd be a pretty penny to those as took ye back t' yer mama," the sweet-voiced person commented. They glanced at Thony. "Both o' ye. Though I s'ppose yer *ugly servant with the speech problem* will be put to some punishment fer 'elpin' ye."

Daffyd paled quite realistically. Possibly that was because it *was* a real reaction. "Don't – please. I really *will* be forced to marry an old woman if I stay."

The tall boy snorted. "Like it matters t' such as us. Ye'll still be a prince and live in the lap o' luxury the whiles we scrape fer crusts an' a spot t' sleep."

"Let me go and you'll earn the favor of my sister," Daffyd said a little desperately. "And... and my Môthir. The Princess-Heir. They don't want to see me go into this marriage."

"Then let *them* stop it," the sweet-voiced person said in a testing tone. "If they cain't – or *won't* – that must mean 'tis the Queen's will. 'Druther have *her* favor *now* fer returnin' ye than *mebbe* a favor *someday* from a woman as *might* be our next queen."

Hard to argue with that... though why the hesitation over who would be the next queen?

"'Druther have the favor o' the Commander-General, too," the person continued. "See more'a *her* than royalty. Or her people anyways. City Guard Commander answers to the General, aye?"

Daffyd's posture was beginning to slump in defeat...

Thony sighed. He had some options here, but Puck – Skiftglow – had definitely meant for him to take Daffyd with him. And if they weren't to be hunted by the Queen's – or the Commander-General's – forces all the way up the mountains, they needed to do it *discreetly*.

He wrested an arm free of the thoroughly distracted street-kids holding onto him and pushed his own hood back, tugging his veil down to hang around his neck. The sudden blaze of his hair attracted everyone's attention nearly as much as his movements.

A murmur of *'the foreign prince'* ran around the group. The sweet-voiced person gave Thony a curious look, then ran their gaze over Daffyd in an *appraising* way.

"Except *you* can't turn him over, can you?" Thony asked, not bothering to try to mimic Daffyd's accent anymore. He gave the sweet-voiced person a direct look. "You'll have to get some of your crew to do it for you. Like Rissa there, maybe?"

He got a glower in return. "And what would *you* know about it, foreigner?"

Thony gave the person back a wry look. "Because in the eyes of the City Guards – and probably their Commander – *I'm* less strange than you are. Aren't I?" He gave them a cool look. "It doesn't matter to *me*. I have other friends like you. But since you can't turn Prince Daffyd in on your own – just *who* is going to be owed the favor? *Or* the 'pretty penny'?"

The person drew themselves up a bit as their crew made some restless movements without really changing positions. Thony kept his gaze meeting that of the leader, reminding himself that he'd helped defeat an evil sorcerer and a Dark-elf just a couple of months ago. And that he was on his way to visit with a Goddess.

This was just a street-kid. And one with a problem almost as big as they were.

Pathremir... didn't really value diversity, after all. And just as in Flowerdust *(which seemed fine with other kinds of diversity)*, people who straddled the line between male and female – or chose to cross the line entirely – were the ones least accepted. Skylir – and a few others in the crew – had had Jost's protection. And Jost himself had offered it because *he* 'leaned the other way,' as they put it around here.

This person in front of them now had unquestionably won their place as leader of this crew with their fists – and then retained it by their wits. None of the others here were of sufficient size to challenge them... individually, and Thony's understanding of such challenges was that they were one-on-one. But if the redheaded prince was reading the situation right, they trusted their crew about as far as they could throw them.

So, about five or six feet, tops.

Trust them to turn in the prince to the Guards, get a fair reward in cash and future favors... and then *turn it over* to their leader? Almost certainly not. You could practically see the wheels churning behind Rissa's weaselly face.

But as long as this person retained their control over the crew... they were the one to deal with.

It hadn't been *all* that different for Jost, after all. Except that Jost's *differences* could be hidden if he chose, and this person's soprano voice probably couldn't mimic a manly tenor. Nor did their body-type allow them to affect a feminine shape and posture. They were trapped, neither hen nor rooster to outside perceptions, always to be discriminated against before anyone bothered to look deeper to find out who they were on the *inside*.

Thony hoped his empathy for the person's situation shone out the way he was trying to project it. He'd been thinking a great deal more about *spells* these last few months since dealing with Valderon Raven'sWing... and wrestling with the good and bad of using his own natural abilities. Proper royalty of the Mountain-Region *had* the ability to use magick, but it was considered utterly gauche to use it for anything more than self-defense against a magickal threat – and some actually abjured the use even then.

It seemed to be thought of very differently here on Amanita's world.

King Mithral of Selavan and his Queen used their magick quite profligately, in Thony's opinion. Unlit lanterns and torches filled the rooms the king might frequent simply so that his 'presence' could light them and they would dim and die in his absence.

For Mithral, that took as much effort as Thony imagined it would for him to do himself, and he'd been mightily impressed with the stamina that the king needed to keep up this popular fantasy to support his claim of being their God's Chosen Disciple. Apparently, Mithral *had* been rather dramatically Chosen from among his brothers and cousins to be Selavan's King, but their Lord of Light didn't seem to have spent much effort on him since, to judge by how worn the king looked.

Queen Lochea's Presence really *did* seem to light up the room – and it didn't really require lamps and candles. The Goddess of Light and Darkness *and* the Lord of Light had Chosen *her*, and imbued the young woman with some of the Goddess' Own Power, it seemed.

And this 'Goddess of Light and Darkness' was also the Silver Dragon Goddess of Pathremir, according to Puck, who should know if anyone did. So, presumably the Pathremiri royalty also had powers. Amanita had implied as much a while back, though Thony didn't remember ever seeing her use any of it.

And there had been all kinds of crazy magick in use at the Court in Dysacha. Mostly to create those ridiculous, overdone costumes they all wore, as far as Thony could tell.

The royalty of Brelsin – in which Flowerdust had been located – and the other one-horse flatland countries he had passed through with the Pathremiri contingent on the way here had seemed more like jumped up mayoral families than Lineages that Held the Divine Right of Kings. Unsurprisingly, there hadn't been hardly any detectable magick in any of them; Commander Zaja had just had them ride on through and stay at local inns without bothering to have Amanita and Daffyd *(and Thony)* go through the rigamarole of making a State Visit to any of them.

(Thony rather appreciated the notion of a 'one-horse-country' after traveling across those Central Plains. The idea was that the country wasn't any larger than the distance a man on a horse could ride in a single day. It was descriptive and gave a very clear idea of the size of the place.)

*(Amanita had referred to some of the towns they'd passed through as 'one-horse-towns,' which was something else entirely. She'd used the term derogatorily – and even when there were multiple locally-owned equines within sight – to suggest that the places were too small to have more than one horse. Which actually made no sense to Thony. Villages and smaller towns that had more of an agricultural basis seemed to have **more** horses, rather than fewer, at least in his experience so far.)*

Anyways, there were clearly a variety of different viewpoints regarding the use of magick.

Valderon Raven'sWing's massive use of *compulsion* spells to control thousands of people and turn them into drooling zombies *(well, Thony hadn't actually seen any of them **drooling**... and storybook zombies were undead and tried to eat people... so technically the enspelled folk hadn't actually been 'zombies')* was clearly over the line. So was Raven'sWing's use of love spells – that one had bit him in the butt when the spell failed and Stillheart broke the Binding that had kept Raven'sWing alive.

But the Light of Queen Lochea's Presence involved a sort of *compulsion* spell as well, and that seemed to be Divinely Approved.

Thony.... right now was trying to walk a very fine line between trying to let this... *gender-ambiguous person* in front of him understand that he sympathized and respected them through all the means that any relatively charismatic commoner might use...

... and with casting a very low-level *compulsion* spell to do the same thing.

And he was discovering – to his dismay – that it was almost second-nature for him to push it all the way over the line.

Daffyd was giving him a weird look...

But something in the street-kid-chieftain's eyes was softening. Or no, not *softening,* there was nothing *soft* about this person. But... *believing,* maybe.

"So, foreign prince," they said, rocking back on their heels and folding their arms. "What d'ye think ye can offer 'at's better?" He nodded at the ones holding Thony from behind and they let him go.

Thony didn't take a breath of relief – the rest of this crew was restless and looking like they didn't really agree with their chief yielding even as much as this. But he'd learned a few things from Jost's crew beyond how to hide his money from pickpockets.

Or... he'd better hope he had.

The redheaded prince tilted his head, letting his gaze sweep the entire group that lay within his field of vision. He didn't smile, but gave them serious, respectful attention.

"I'm a prince in my homeland, it's true. But I ran with a crew of street-kids for awhile. Down on the Central Plains. A little town called Flowerdust. Just happened to be where a certain Evil Wizard – name of Raven'sWing – was collecting all his thousands of enspelled troops. He planned to take over the Fairy Wood and then conquer... well, everywhere."

Thony met all the eyes that he could, again.

"S'what 'appened?" someone demanded after a moment of silence.

The redheaded prince shrugged. "We stopped him. Me and the street-kids – their chieftain's name was Jost," he added. "Oh, and Princess Amanita was part of our crew."

It was harder to be nonchalant about Jost. He missed the other boy rather fiercely at that moment, and not just because of the current predicament. Jost would have been a tremendous traveling companion. Daffyd... looked to need a lot of taking care of.

The impudent Rissa snorted. "Ye ain't tellin' us the *Princess* ran with street-rats. Nor you neither. I won' b'lieve it." She glanced around the group, carefully *not* looking at her leader. "Nany one of you as *does* ain't smart enough to know which end o'... a cup to drink outta!"

Thony was sort of amused to notice how she paused at the end there, glancing back and forth between him and Daffyd. And then quickly substituted that thing about the cup for whatever – and presumably *ruder* thing she would normally have said. Apparently, Rissa didn't want to look poorly in front of her prince, even if she 'didn't believe' Thony.

The redheaded prince gave a nonchalant shrug. "It's up to you, of course. I can't *make* you believe what I tell you."

His phrasing was – unintentionally – a parallel to what he'd been telling Daffyd a few minutes ago, and he glanced at the Pathremiri prince. Daffyd looked... anxious but holding it together.

"It's really a matter of whether you want to support a future Queen who *knows* street-kids because she's lived like one... or a future Queen controlled by the Eldest-Princess. And having met both of them – I can tell you that while Amanita is annoying as all get out, Reyalla is one scary, um... *witch*."

And Thony let his eyes flicker again to Daffyd after his own brief hesitation to make it pretty clear that he was doing the same thing Rissa had.

Of course he didn't know these guys like Rissa did, so putting in a word *he* was more likely to use like *'lady'* probably wouldn't work here.

Thony didn't generally use crude language himself *(early attempts on his part having been dealt with in the typical way for the Mountain-Region: his nurse had washed his mouth out with soap.*

Joanna had stopped her from doing that later on, but the Point Had Been Made as far as he was concerned) but he'd hung out with the stableboys in Aldyrwald and then Jost's crew enough to have access to a fairly extensive vocabulary.

The sweet-voiced person whose name Thony still hadn't heard narrowed their eyes. "Ye're ain't *offerin'* us summat. Ye're *askin'* more-a us. Ye're *askin'* 'at we go outta our way to support Princess Amanita. *And* 'er mum, I suppose?"

Thony inclined his head to agree with that interpretation.

"An' no real gain for us outta all this," they finished.

Thony spread his hands. "She's young and not in charge. But so are all of you. I know it's hard to plan for the long-term when you live on the streets–"

"Like, *impossible,*" someone muttered.

Thony flashed a grin in the direction of the mutter. "Some of that's choice. You're a big crew. You've got places you hide out. You split the take to make sure everyone gets *something* even on the bad days. Jost looked for ways to get his crew into real apprenticeships or at least *jobs* as they got too old to manage on the streets – I imagine you do that, too. Even if everyone has to go short for awhile to save up the fees."

He looked around at them. "A good crew is a family. And families do more than look after each other through thick and thin. They plan ahead to make the future better than the present."

That... seemed to have caught their imagination.

Daffyd was giving him a weird look again.

Rissa was standing on tiptoe and whispering fiercely at the ear of the huge person with that sweet voice and her tall boyfriend was listening. The others had clumped up a bit and were muttering to each other and looking at, well, *Thony* as if they couldn't quite bear not to.

Thony tried to radiate relaxed confidence.

Unfortunately, Daffyd looked like he was gathering himself to bolt...

And if he actually tried, that would undo everything that had been accomplished so far...

Rather like his sister setting the Raven HQ on fire and messing everything up after Thony had talked himself and Dae out of the rat-/mouse-impersonation thing...

Thony found himself dithering about whether to *nudge* things along a bit before he didn't have the chance to do so. But that would mean he'd have to cross that line a bit farther... which if he didn't *have* to...

The large ambiguously-gendered person looked up right then from listening to Rissa and stepped forwards. They bowed cordially to Daffyd, who had the sense to nod regally, but then they turned to Thony and walked forwards, offering him a hand.

"I'm Dell," they said as Thony took the hand with a hopefully-just-right-firm grasp of his own. "Let's go somewhere and chat about this some more."

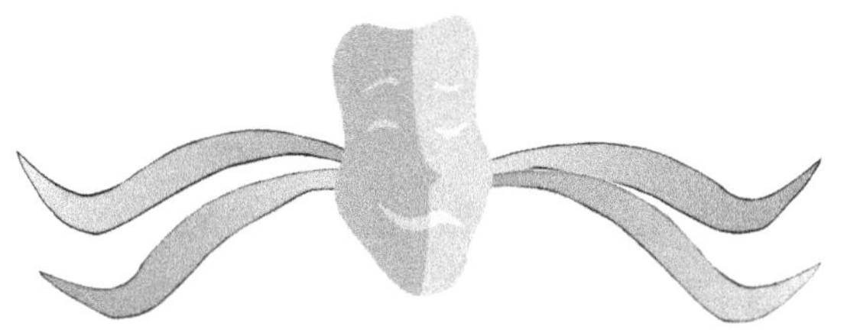

Chapter SIX

Beyond Understanding

"P HEW," DAFFYD SAID AS THE sun set and their mounts cantered easily across the flat plain towards the mountains rising sharply to the west. "I wasn't sure we'd get out of there *alive,* and then you... I'm, *still* not sure what you did. It didn't *feel* like you used anything... *extra...?*"

Thony was in a fairly good mood at this point. It had taken them hours longer than expected to reach the meeting-point where Twinklestar and the horses waited for them.

First there was there was the time to negotiate with Dell and for Daffyd to write a letter of introduction to Amanita. And then it took even longer because Dell and Rissa had insisted that they pull their robes and veils back on for the remainder of the journey *and* that the crew would give them a full escort to ensure they made it there safely.

It had been... a little odd being treated like... well, like a *precious princess* the way he'd expect everyone to treat his sisters or Roger's sisters or something.

But it got the job done and he didn't have a deadline on how long it was supposed to take them to get anywhere. So long as Skiftglow was able to distract and redirect pursuit, they'd have plenty of a headstart.

And because they *hadn't* told Dell and the rest about Thony being a unicorn-maiden, Twinklestar had stayed back from sight until they were alone and Thony had 'perforce' had to ride Silverfoot. And there wasn't any particular reason to switch back for the short bit of distance they'd be able to make tonight, so he was *still* riding Silverfoot. Whose paces *didn't* feel like taking a poorly-sprung wagon over broken ground.

But to answer Daffyd's question...

"No," he said only half-honestly. Apparently, he hadn't used enough of that *extra* for Daffyd to be able to tell, and... that was good enough, wasn't it? "I didn't need to. Street-kids are like everyone else, Daffyd. They just want someone to care about what happens to them – and have a safe place to live, decent food to eat, and a future to look forwards to. Amanita and I learned that in Flowerdust, so all I needed to do was convince Dell and the rest that we really *had*. And that she *would*."

Gods, but he really, really hoped she *would*.

He'd had Daffyd write his sister a letter in the secret code the two of them had been using since they were little kids, explaining the whole thing.

Well, most of the whole thing.

It explained that the bearer of the note – who might be Rissa or the tall, slender girl they actually *called* Willow and who apparently cleaned up well – represented Dell and their crew. And that – in return for a fairly modest retainer – the crew would be her eyes and ears on the streets. And, if need be, her secret escape route.

The retainer fee was just enough for the crew to be able to give up petty thievery to keep themselves fed and housed. Thony had suggested that Daffyd mention that Amanita might want to supplement that so they could slowly replace worn out clothing items and so on. Regardless of whether she did or not, it meant that *this* crew wouldn't end up with being all-too-recognizable to the City Guards for all the wrong reasons. That would make them more anonymous, and therefore more useful to their princess.

Thony suspected that this extra bit of prosperity would attract more kids to the crew, making them even more useful to Amanita and her family.

And – once she could figure out how to get away from her royal duties for a bit – it would give her a chance to see the underside of her city. The grotty, ugly parts that weren't triaged and prettied up for royal viewing... and that Daffyd was clearly still having trouble with.

After all the things he'd seen and done recently, Thony was convinced that could only be to the good.

He'd do the same once he got home – not that he was sure there was a grotty underbelly to Aldyrwald. But he'd never even been to the far side of the home-valley; never been to the other two valleys at all; never roamed the forests and mountain-sides; never explored the passes... never visited the neighboring kingdoms.

There probably were people in his land who *were* poor and struggling, though it wasn't likely there was much in the way of a local equivalent to street-kids. There really weren't *streets,* after all. Flowerdust had been five or ten times the size of both home-villages put together and the reports he'd read were that the other two valleys only had one village each.

Though Papa's noble vassals all had their estates in the foothills as well, and the people living on each of *those* might well add up to another village – which added up to... a fair number more people. But they were all still spread out in little clumps, not gathered together in towns and cities. *(Or maybe that should be **a** town or a city... given the numbers involved.)*

No, Aldyrwald's poor people were probably scraping their livings out of forest plants and mountain berries. Or possibly on the estates of the nobles, since some of them seemed to forever be on the verge of financial disaster and so surely weren't taking good care of the peasants beholden to them.

The less-well-off families in the valley villages might be short on the few luxuries that everyone else around them had, but they weren't starving and their kids ganging up to rob the very rare random stranger. Truly desperate forest-boys and valley-girls might grow up to be bandits, but there hadn't even been *bandits* in Aldyrwald's mountains in generations.

"You're a strange lad, Thony," Daffyd commented, and Thony looked over to see the older prince shaking his head.

"What do you mean?" Thony asked.

"You're all ready to defend these street-kids – but you have no empathy whatsoever for the 'middleborn' princesses and princes in your homeland." Daffyd shook his head again, glancing at Thony before restoring his attention to the dusky road ahead.

They were heading towards the west, so the shadows of the peaks in front of them had already enveloped the travelers, despite the sky still being bright just above them.

"That's not true," Thony exclaimed, surprised and a little hurt by the accusation. "Some of my best friends are middleborns."

Well, Roger was anyways. And he'd liked his uncles when they'd stopped by to visit. And Aunt Rosabel, who usually came along when Mama's parents visited.

"Name some," Daffyd prodded, and Thony glared at him and named Roger.

"So, *one*," the Pathremiri prince noted. "Have you even *talked* to any others?"

"My uncles and aunt," Thony told him. "The neighbors weren't exactly jumping all over themselves to socialize with us, not since I put frogs in all their stuff after Joanna's sixteenth birthday party."

"You *what?*" Daffyd was startled enough that he inadvertently jerked on the reins and his horse stumbled a little. He soothed her before turning his incredulous gaze on the Crown Prince of Aldyrwald. "You put frogs in the luggage of the visiting royals at your own *sister's* party?"

"I was only five," Thony said defensively. "I hadn't really developed a great deal in the way of subtlety yet."

Daffyd blinked. "Um, *not* what I meant..."

"I know what you meant." Thony looked straight ahead, ignoring Twinklestar's concerned look and soothing comments in the back of his head.

He'd managed to talk around this with Daffyd so far.

Amanita knew, of course, since she'd been in Aldyrwald. But he had asked her not to share about Prissy's tail with anyone.

It wasn't that Prissy's tail embarrassed him. It was just that Thony knew, from painful experience, that not everyone accepted things like a perfect, golden-haired princess bearing tails. That tail was, after all, the reason the neighbors had decided that the Devinthal Line had lost the Divine Right of Kings and Thony had needed to run off in the first place.

Well, to be utterly honest, it wasn't *just* Prissy's tail.

It was also the fact that his parents hadn't managed a proper number of children.

And the centaur herd that had returned home with his sisters from their Quest.

And all the 'weird rumors' beginning to float around about how Princess Joanna and Princess Priscilla – and even *Prince Roger* of *Schwannsberg,* who should be a more proper sort – were actually *using magick powers,* even though everyone knew royalty *shouldn't.*

"Jo is eleven years older than me," Thony began and went on to explain about Prissy being born nine years later and her bushy, black tail, *(and the stupid appellations that had gotten stuck on him and both his sisters – 'Affable and Affirmative,'* **sheesh!***)* and the trouble it had made with the neighbors. And how his sisters couldn't find husbands, so they went on the Husband-Hunting Quest, but instead they came back with an explanation for the tail. *(Long story short, but it had come to her from a tribe of beings called 'Perushin' who stored their magick in their tails, transferring a tail from elder to newborn... and Prissy's – the oldest and most magickal of them all – had been thought lost...).*

And Twinklestar and the centaurs had come along – because Twinklestar had wanted to bond with Prissy but she'd fallen in love with the young centaur stallion, Jeremy.

And Roger and Joanna said they'd gotten married along the way – but Mama and Papa and Roger's parents had insisted on re-doing the ceremony 'to save face.' Jo had already been pregnant, she had told them... she'd just barely begun to show before Thony had left.

And a wizard and sorceress – Phillip and Cythera, who were also married to each other – had come home with them, too.

And Roger and Joanna and Phillip and Cythera and Prissy had all become Gods and Goddesses after a scary, cloudless night when all the stars went dark and apparently all their *old* Gods and Goddesses had died. And it had been impossible to miss because Joanna's Sacred Mountain as Goddess of Earth had suddenly appeared and engulfed the back half of the Devinthals' castle. And Roger had been sitting and having a brandy with Papa and Great-Uncle Sir Eddie and had suddenly vanished in a *whoosh* of wind.

To the other side of the world, it had turned out. Where Roger, as God of Air, had an ever-churning Sacred Whirlwind.

And Cythera and Phillip had vanished from their guestroom at the same time. They had been whisked away – in a gout of flame and a spontaneous rain shower, neither of which had left a mark – they told everyone when they reappeared in time for the re-do of Roger and Joanna's nuptials. Cythera had ended up with a Sacred Palace of Flame and Phillip with a Sacred Whirlpool.

"They called it a *Ragnarök*," Thony concluded as he scraped together some dinner for them while Daffyd laid out bedrolls. Twinklestar had found them a good campsite while he'd been giving his looooong explanation. "It means something about a changeover of–"

"I know what it means," Daffyd said as he sat down on his spread-out bedroll and regarded Thony with bemusement. "It's part of the Líonar Old Tongue... and since we thought that was what had happened to *our* Goddesses for so long, it became part of ours, too."

"Because They weren't responding when you prayed to them?" Thony asked, testing the bacon in the frying pan. He'd learned to cook a *little* bit on the ride through the Fairy Wood, and then a tiny bit more under Jost's supervision in Flowerdust.

Cooking bacon still made him nervous, though.

Daffyd nodded. "All right, that explains about your Quest, I suppose. And maybe even how this pranking around of yours got started–"

Thony had made sure to explain how the neighbors had made fun of Prissy at Joanna's party and pulled her tail and there really hadn't been anything *else* he could do to protect her as a brother should. And how more or less the same thing had happened nine years later at Prissy's own 'coming out' party – and eldest-born princess or not, Jo hadn't had so much as a single suitor besides Roger, who hadn't dared to flout tradition *(then)* and actually court her officially. *(And how **that** time, Thony had pranked **all** the royal visitors at Jo's **request,** to camouflage her sneaking off with Prissy and Roger on the Husband-Hunting Quest.)*

"–and I can see you're fond of this Roger-person," Daffyd went on. "But that still doesn't explain how you can be so callous about the fates of all those middleborns but so sympathetic to the street-kids. Especially the ones who..."

He let his voice trail off and Thony glanced up from flipping the finished bacon onto a plate to see the older boy duck his head.

Oh. So, *that* was what this was all about.

"You're still grumpy with me because of your part in the negotiations," Thony stated, trying not to laugh.

"I am *not*," Daffyd grumped. "Though I don't see why that had to be a part of what you offered them. Or why *you* couldn't do it."

Thony grinned. "*I'm* just a foreigner claiming to be a prince. From Dell's perspective, I could be *anyone*, really. But *you* matter to her. Besides, I thought you told me you 'like kissing people'?"

Between the darkness, the ruddy glow of the campfire, and Daffyd's dark skin, it was next to impossible to tell if he was blushing.

Dell hadn't so much explained away her perceptible gender-ambiguity as Thony had come to the realization that you'd have to be crazy *not* to choose to be a girl in Pathremir if there was any question about it – girls were the people with all the power after all. So, he'd taken a chance and addressed the street-kid-chieftain as 'Miss Dell' – and gotten a beaming smile and a great deal more cooperation in response.

Luck, of course. It *could* have gone the other way. People weren't always logical the way logic made sense to Thony.

He's blushing, Twinklestar commented wickedly into Thony's mind. The unicorn was across the little bit of meadowland where they had stopped for the night, grazing peaceably beside the horses, the shimmer of his white hide somehow muted. *I can tell.*

"Twinklestar says you're blushing," Thony informed his friend archly.

"You would be, too, if you'd had to kiss that, that *she-male,*" Daffyd snarled back.

Oops. Too much pushing, apparently.

And... how disappointing that this was where *Daffyd's* compassion apparently came to die.

"I'd've happily kissed Dell if that's what she wanted," Thony handed the Pathremiri prince a plate with bacon and roughly cut bread and a small pot of honey to drizzle on it.

Daffyd narrowed his eyes at him. "You're a *pragmatic* sort, aren't you, Thony?"

"She didn't want more money, and it won *your* sister better spies than she could've afforded–"

"*Some* things are more important than *money,*" Daffyd looked mortally offended as he poured out honey. "If I'd thought I could get out of there safely and go home and leave you to your... your *machinations* right then, I'd've done it."

Thony raised his eyebrows, taking the pot back and treating his own bread. "Really? Right back into your lovely Commander-General's arms?"

Daffyd winced automatically, then shook himself to glower at Thony again. "Better than dealing with that *unnatural creature.*"

Thony gave him a dark look. "Dell's an admirable person, Daffyd. She can't help how her body has turned out – and she shouldn't be made to feel bad about it. We're all just the way the Gods made us to be. Do you want to argue with the *Gods?*"

"And you'd've *'happily kissed'* that thing," Daffyd sneered. "When you weren't so *happy* to kiss *me.*"

Was this... *jealousy?*

Or was it really that reactive *(and unattractive)* intolerance Thony had already seen too much of amongst the people of Pathremir?

The women-warriors and the Eldest-Princess, but also the shopkeepers and such along the ride to the Queen's City. Back in Flowerdust, Commander Zaja had barely been able to make herself speak to Davril or Istevan, and she'd ignored the existence of Skylir entirely, though she had done nearly the same with all the street-kids, so it hadn't stood out, terribly.

Thony had had higher hopes for Amanita's closer-kin – the people that *she* liked and respected *(though **she** hadn't really had a problem with Commander Zaja, other than not wanting to be in someone else's charge).* He'd had nothing but positive interactions with the Queen and Princess-Heir and Prince Naeel. And Daffyd...

Gods, he sure hoped this little... temper tantrum *was* jealousy.

That 'green-eyed monster' couldn't possibly be as ugly as... whatever one might call this other thing.

Of course, Daffyd *had* kissed Dell when it was asked of him.

And Thony had seen enough people kissing to know that the Pathremiri prince had given good measure for his effort. And *Dell* had certainly been pleased afterwards.

Maybe it didn't matter what Daffyd had or hadn't been thinking on the inside if he did all the right things on the outside.

Well.

Maybe not to Dell, who would likely never know. *(And who had, after all, gotten to kiss a handsome prince. Which was more than most any other poor girl might be able to say she'd done.)*

But it mattered to *Thony*.

Thony decided to play this for all it was worth... and pray he wouldn't see worse instead of better. He wasn't really sure he could bear to travel with someone – to be *friends* with someone – who saw a living, breathing, thinking person and didn't treat them like a person.

He fluttered his eyelashes at Daffyd – who was glowering fiercely and directly at him, so he shouldn't miss seeing that, even in the semi-dark. "I never said I wasn't *happy* about it, Daffyd."

Which at least had the salutary effect of breaking that glower and turning the older boy's expression back to something closer to *bemused*.

Bemused... and then... *despairing?*

"It doesn't matter anymore. It's not like *that's* ever happening again. Now." Daffyd brightened slightly. "Hey! That's something I hadn't thought about. If Taeryl finds out, *she* won't want to kiss me *either!*"

He paused, stroking the sides of his smooth chin thoughtfully as Thony frowned over *that*.

"No," Daffyd added after a moment. "There's no way to let her find out without putting Dell and her buddies into danger. Not worth it."

Thony felt his frown deepen. "Into *danger?* Isn't that overstating it? I mean, I know your people think people can't fall in love with someone of their own gender..."

Daffyd looked startled. "What? No. No one thinks *that*."

Thony raised an eyebrow and mentioned his observation of Commander Zaja's interaction with Istevan and Davril.

Daffyd actually laughed. "Oh. That. No, that was all about the two of them being a pair and raising a baby without a *woman.* Men here aren't considered to have legal standing – we can't own property or businesses or anything. So, a family without a woman in it is going to have problems just existing. I mean, she may have some *personal* distaste for the idea, but I don't think she – or any of the women with her – doubted that Istevan and Davril were in love."

He smiled a little wistfully. "That was pretty obvious."

"So, pairs of *women* aren't a problem?" Thony asked to clarify things.

Daffyd shook his head. "I mean, it's sort of *frowned* upon, because you need a guy around to have babies and it's every woman's duty to provide herself with heirs."

Thony gave him an utterly baffled look. "Then what's the problem with you kissing Dell? Either she's a girl – and that's who she is, regardless of what's inside her pants – or she's a boy and you've clearly never had a problem with doing *that.*"

"Safer to kiss boys anyways," Daffyd muttered, his cheeks darkening again in the firelight, so presumably he was blushing again. "No chance of being tricked into taking it farther and ending up with a wife I didn't want. Well. Ending up with a wife I didn't want *accidentally.*"

The look on his face suggested he'd considered that very idea as an alternative to marrying the Commander-General. And that his sense of responsibility had stopped him. Just as with a princess – a *non-middleborn* princess – in the Mountain-Region, Daffyd's marriage was meant to be coin that his Grandmother-the-Queen, or his mother in her turn, would spend for the good of the Realm.

Not that it was so different for even an *eldest-born prince* of the Mountain-Region, as Thony knew all too well. He just spent a little differently.

Presumably it was the same deal for Amanita.

"So, then what's the problem with Dell?" Thony asked again. "She's a nice person. Extremely responsible. Obviously pretty sharp. A leader that others follow willingly." All big pluses in Thony's book. "And you said Taeryl knowing about that kiss would put her in *danger?*"

Daffyd sighed. "If... *she* were trying to live as a boy it wouldn't be *quite* as much of a problem. There are laws – and a great deal of, um, *public distaste* – for people who don't clearly fit as a man or a woman. A boy or a girl. Or, who, um, appear to be trying to *switch.*"

Thony raised his eyebrows. "Laws?"

This time his friend winced. "Yeah. Punishable by public flogging. Or imprisonment. Or hard labor. They haven't been enforced in generations – but the laws still exist. And people like Grandmother-the-Eldest-Princess and Taeryl keep Grandmother-the-Queen from removing them entirely. There was a whole *thing* going on about that shortly before I left to go look for Amanita. Môthir and Vathir have gone through our laws and are advocating for getting rid of ones that don't seem terribly useful anymore."

He rolled his eyes. "The laws of this country fill up an entire set of volumes. *Thick* books. *Lots* of them. And the precedent and commentary on them fills up an entire small room. There's an entire profession devoted just to memorizing them for use in the legal courts, and at least two printing presses that I'm aware of that stay in business just by producing copies of all of it for the lawyers and their staffs."

"That could make sense," Thony allowed, trying not to look as boggled as he felt.

Aldyrwald's 'legal system' came down to Papa's decision.

Oh, there were volumes of precedent stored in the castle, and the king *usually* referred to that in complicated situations. Thony had been required to study those case histories – which had been pretty interesting stuff and he'd read through them avidly for a couple of years.

But in the end, the king could do pretty much as he chose. His nobles could do pretty much as *they* chose on their estates, though their peasants could appeal to Papa. And the village magistrates handled minor infractions of the peace and sent anything else up to their local liege-lord – which was Papa for the home-villages.

There wasn't really anything *codifying* how it was all supposed to be done. Nor were there any such written *laws* elsewhere in the Mountain-Region, as far as Thony knew. He rather thought one of Uncle Louis' letters had mentioned something about 'legal proceedings' in a 'court' a few years ago, but it hadn't made a great deal of sense at the time.

Now that Thony had seen large cities – and the almost inconceivable numbers of people who lived in them – that old missive made more sense. A king – or queen – couldn't possibly handle all the grievances of a city the size of the Queen's City, let alone Dysacha or Dynsfyor, even if they only handled the most major ones. And if they did those, there were still some ten times as many minor issues; he'd listened when the village-magistrates and noblemen made reports to Papa and had realized that years ago.

And, he supposed, if someone else was dispensing justice in the king's name, you'd want to give them guidelines.

*(And none of that even touched on what he thought of **printing presses**... Everything had to be hand-copied in Aldyrwald, though there were a handful of printed books in the Royal Library that Master Esquith had deemed too delicate and precious for Thony to touch. Which, of course, meant that he'd snuck in to read them on his own time.*

*(Which... had been a little disappointing, honestly. You'd think if you were setting up to be able to make dozens of copies of something, you'd make sure it was something **interesting** that you were printing. But noooo. There had been a manual on modern techniques of horse-breeding, and a cookbook, and some old guy's dissertation on why rich people should be in charge of everything because they had more of a chance to be educated. Which, well **duh**.*

*(At least that one had made Thony have to think for awhile. He'd decided he didn't hold with this dude's notion of 'Philosopher-Kings.' People like the stablemaster, Tad, might possibly be better at ruling than Papa if they only had the chance to study all the things that Thony had been forced to do. Not that he had been sure what one could **do** about that distinction until he'd seen the public library in Dynsfyor.*

*(Though... he – the Devinthals – had a responsibility to the people of Aldyrwald, as manifested in the Divine Right of Kings. That had been drilled into Thony since birth. If you rearranged everything so that the cleverest peasants could learn as much as they wanted and **they** started ruling things... could you make sure they paid attention to everyone's needs, even if they weren't clever and educated? The Philosopher-King dude's ideas suggested maybe **not...** and **that** suggested that letting that happen would be abrogating his family's responsibilities?*

*(Except why **wouldn't** they be at least as good at looking after everyone as a king-by-inheritance...? There were some pretty bad kings out there... It was enough to make Thony's head hurt.)*

Daffyd nodded at him as if Thony's boggled silence had been a thoughtful comment.

"Anyways, the Eldest-Princess and the General Staff of the Army – led by Commander-General Taeryl – objected to the removal of the gender-clarity laws. Strongly. And when most of the more conservative older noblewomen supported them, Grandmother-the-Queen had to back down."

He gave Thony a wry look. "Vathir told me that Môthir plans to deal with it when *she* is Queen... and after all the old fogies have passed their titles on. She thinks the next generation will be more open-minded."

"But that's not going to be for a *really* long time," Thony concluded. "Your Grandmother – either of them – aren't really all that old. Objectively speaking."

Daffyd sighed and shook his head. "No. And I wouldn't want anything bad to happen to... um, either of them. I suppose." He winced. "That's the whole basis of this thing about me marrying Taeryl. She's *really* old to have another child, but she's healthy and being Commander-General keeps her in great shape. And I'm sure they have the best Healers in the Realm available to her."

Thony frowned. "I *really* don't understand how your Court works. At home, Papa makes decisions and no one else gets to argue. But here the Eldest-Princess has a... a *faction* and can make the *ruling Queen* change her decision when she doesn't want to. "

Daffyd tilted his head. "Your father didn't want to have to make you get married early, but he was going to do it anyways, wasn't he?"

"That's different," Thony objected. "That's because the neighbors would use their armies to..."

His voice trailed off as Daffyd gave him a wry look.

"But Aldyrwald and the surrounding countries aren't just *factions* within one *Court,*" Thony objected, though the parallels made his objection rather... faint. "They're separate and independent countries!"

Daffyd shrugged. "I haven't been there, so I can't really say. And – to get back to where we started this – Taeryl probably wouldn't refuse to marry me because I'd kissed Dell. But she'd be mortally offended and throw the full weight of the law against Dell. And then I'd have to live the rest of my life not just as that woman's husband, but with her scorn."

He hesitated. "And I'm sure I'd *never* get to even *see* my daughter outside of official settings."

There was a long moment with only the crackling of the campfire for sound. Even Twinklestar was quiet in Thony's head, though the redheaded prince was aware that the unicorn had been listening closely to their conversation.

"So..." he said at last, "you weren't *personally bothered* by Dell? Just... the potential repercussions?"

Daffyd winced. "And I didn't particularly want to have to kiss a stranger. *Another* stranger. I get quite enough of that at home, thank you very much." He slanted a somewhat furtive look at Thony. "I get your point about Dell being the person the Gods made... *her* out to be. It still seems... wrong and unnatural to me. But she shouldn't be treated as if she weren't a person. Or discriminated against."

Thony thought about that. Was it enough to want to treat everyone fairly, even if you felt differently on the inside?

"And I still think your attitudes about 'middleborns' – and *women* – are a little bizarre," Daffyd added, looking at Thony a little more directly.

"*Women?*" Thony exclaimed, shaken out of his ruminations. "What do you mean by *that?*"

Daffyd snorted. "It's getting late. I don't think I have the energy to argue with you about *another* topic."

He set his plate next to the fire and laid down in his bedroll. "Goodnight, Thony."

Thony frowned some more, but Daffyd had turned over and was pretending to be instantly asleep.

With a grumble, he collected the plates and frying pan, scraping off the grease with dry leaves and dumping it in the fire. The smell of bacon again filled the little clearing.

It wasn't the best solution, but Thony was not about to try finding the little stream that ran along the side of their meadow campsite in the dark.

Besides, he'd done the cooking. *(And he hadn't complained about it being women's-work or anything. He had no 'bizarre attitudes' about women.)*

Daffyd could just scrub the stuff up in the morning.

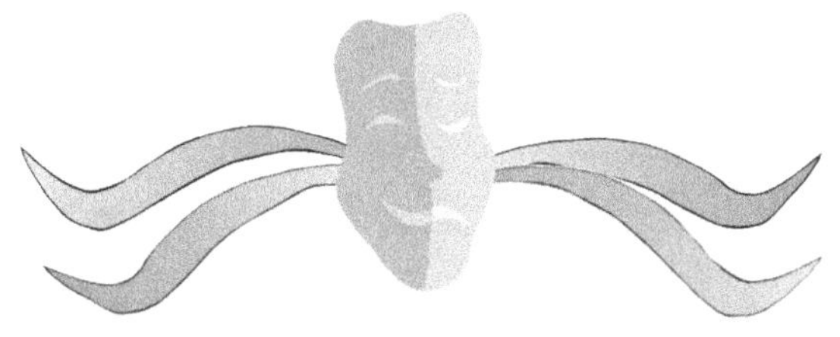

Chapter SEVEN

Meet Cute

DAFFYD HAD TO BE SHOWN how to clean cooking and eating implements, but didn't object to doing so. They got going as early as they could, proceeding farther west towards the mountains.

West, and a little north, and Thony realized they were into some *serious* foothills by mid-day. The rolling hill-country behind the palace had gotten steeper and steeper...

Daffyd – and his showy horse – seemed entirely unfazed by the increasing altitude, but Thony was struggling a bit again, feeling like he needed to breathe harder and faster to get enough air. It was a bit lowering, given that he'd acclimated over the couple of weeks he'd been on the Pathremiri plateau.

"We live up here as much as Môthir and Vathir can get us all away," Daffyd explained when they took a stop. "It was entirely when Amanita and I were little. There's a series of five estates backing right up to the mountains – it's supposed to be enough to have one for each of however-many princesses there are. One is designated for the Princess-Heir – Môthir grew up there, while Grandmother-the-Queen was Princess-Heir. She still prefers it to the palace. I think they both do."

"So, you go this way a lot," Thony summarized. "Should... should we stop in at your home?"

Daffyd looked wistful. "There probably isn't any point. I don't need anything I left there, and the servants might send word that they'd seen us, so it's probably not a good idea." He looked around. "It's probably just luck that we haven't seen anyone else along the road. You don't often see a pair of men traveling alone. Especially *young* men."

Which... was about what Thony might have said about young *women* back in Aldyrwald.

Which made sense, because women were smaller and more delicate and needed to be protected.

Obviously, it was *Daffyd* who had the weird ideas.

Twinklestar snorted, but followed that up with a comment about how it was his doing that they weren't seeing any traffic on this particular road. Exactly *what* he was doing or *how,* he wouldn't explain, but he implied that it was a thing all unicorns knew how to do.

Thony dutifully relayed this, and Daffyd relaxed a little.

"That makes a certain amount of sense," he said. "Unicorns are known for being able to move around without being seen."

They continued on for another hour or so before Daffyd pointed out a quiet country lane breaking away between two hills of mossy rock. The spotty copses of trees and mostly grass had given way a bit ago to spotty meadows surrounded by reasonably dense forest, so the two hills were pretty distinctive.

"That way is home," the Pathremiri prince said. His gaze lingered in the direction of the lane as they passed, but then he turned his eyes resolutely forwards.

He seemed sad, though.

Thony could understand. Daffyd had been gone nearly a year and he'd come back to the glitz and glamour of the palace in the Queen's City. Now he was leaving again, and he hadn't even had time to stop at the place he considered home. It pretty much sucked.

"So, um, if each of the princesses has an estate around here, doesn't that mean your other grandmother has one, too?" he asked after a moment.

Daffyd nodded, eyes still straight ahead. "You don't come this way to find it, though. It's farther to the north. Their other two sisters still live on the other estates. Usually, princesses move out as they have a chance to build their own fortunes and the space is needed for the daughters of the next Queen. But supposedly when Môthir was born, there was... a lot of contention. Supposedly her mother – my grandmother who's now Queen – refused to be wed to, ah, anyone she didn't love. And if that meant she would only ever have the one baby, then so be it."

Thony chuckled. "So that's the other side of the story Puck told us."

His friend winced. "My great-grandmother banished her to this estate until she 'came to her senses.' And told her sisters to lean on her."

*Oh, **that** can't have gone well,* Twinklestar noted and Thony repeated for Daffyd's ears.

"It didn't, particularly," the Pathremiri prince agreed. "The Eldest-Princess was furious already, and the two middle sisters – who are twins and had also been cut out of the succession by Môthir's birth – didn't want to get involved. And Grandmother – Namarina – wasn't willing to listen terribly well anyways."

He sighed. "I suppose at least part of her obstinacy was because Puck was secretly living with them. But I've been treated to lectures on the evils of a stubborn nature from Grandmother-the-Eldest-Princess since we started coming down to the city regularly."

"How long did the banishment last?" Thony asked.

"Until my great-grandmother died and Grandmother Namarina became Queen," Daffyd replied. "When I was a baby."

That seemed a little problematic...

And all that time Namarina was up here in the middle of nowhere, Reyalla was down in the city making contacts and wooing people to her faction? Twinklestar asked, via Thony.

"Not *people*," Daffyd said dryly. "*Noblewomen* of a certain *rank*. She doesn't have much use for anyone else. Though Môthir and Grandmother Namarina *did* have to go down to the city for official duties on a regular basis, Vathir says."

That explains **some** *of the weird relationship between the Eldest-Princess and the Queen,* Twinklestar told Thony. *But not all of it. We're missing something. You don't have to repeat that to Daffyd – he might not even know what's missing.*

Since when do you know all about this stuff? Thony asked.

Twinklestar tilted his head enough for Thony to catch his eye. *Unicorns have politics and power struggles, too, you know. It's not all frolicking in the moonlight and finding beautiful maidens to Bind.*

Well, if that wasn't a little mind-boggling.

Thony decided to ignore the bit about 'beautiful maidens'; that was clearly meant as bait.

Ask him how **his** *parents met,* Twinklestar urged.

That story took up most of the afternoon, for all that it wasn't that involved.

Eldest-Princess Reyalla had left her family up at her hill-country estate and in their father's care most of the time, but left him little to provide for them with. Her royal allowance – which Daffyd assured Thony was quite generous and always had been – was sufficient to cover her lavish lifestyle in the capitol, but she sent no coin or supplies to her husband.

Luckily for the children *(and servants)* the Eldest-Princess had chosen her husband purely based on his physical attractiveness and his family's history of having a large number of girl children. She'd had younger sisters that she had to have a daughter before, after all – not that she'd initially been terribly concerned, since there was seven years between her and the twins, and Namarina had been even younger. She'd taken her time getting around to it... and then lived to make everyone else regret it.

But she'd taken less account of rank – for once – than, um, *fecundity*. So, Prince Naeel's father was a member of the very-much-lesser nobility and had the muscles and form his wife had admired because his family's estate was a farm and he'd been working since he was small.

He'd turned the Eldest-Princess' estate into a working farm, beginning with an extensive vegetable garden, and then expanding to sheep.

"He wanted to raise horses, Vathir said," Daffyd had explained. "Like his own parents did. But he thought it would be too easy for his wife to take all the value of their work away from what he needed to raise his children and maintain the home. Sheep... she only had disdain for."

And *sheep* gave him the excuse to send his son out as a shepherd. Which meant when his mother was visiting, there would be fewer reasons for Prince Naeel to be home. She was awful to all of her family, but especially to the child who had 'failed her' by being born a boy.

"She showed off her pregnancies at Court," Daffyd told them. "*Flaunted* them, since it was a way of showing off how much more of a *woman* she was than her stubborn little sister. And eventually, she took my aunts along with her to show off how many *daughters* she had. Though she sent them home quickly. *Vathir*, she left home entirely."

So, Prince Naeel spent most of his days out with his sheep.

And Princess Ytheril – who'd never had a chance to meet her male cousin – had a habit of escaping to roam the hills and dales of her mother's estate when the two of them would come back from a visit to the Queen's City. Her grandmother – Queen Elegia – had to have them, but spent the whole time comparing Namarina and her sister and disapproving of her oldest granddaughter's quiet ways. After all of that, Princess Ytheril needed a break and would take her sketchbook and colors and find a quiet spot. There were guards on the boundaries of the estate, after all, so she could seek out some real privacy.

"And they just ran into each other out there and had no idea who the other one was," Thony surmised.

He shrugged when Daffyd gave him a startled nod. "Puck told us that he made sure they didn't figure it out until it was, ah, too late."

Daffyd flushed a bit. "So how did *your* parents meet?"

"Oh, just your standard princess-rescue," Thony said blithely. "Mama's parents and Papa's parents had noticed them flirting at a ball, so they discussed it and set it up."

"What's a 'standard princess-rescue'?" Daffyd asked.

Thony shrugged one shoulder. He'd always loved the story of Mama and Papa's courtship – his grandparents had put some real effort into giving them a unique story, after all, and he'd been sure his own would do the same. Which clearly was never going to happen now.

"Grandpa Dave contracted with a witch to kidnap Mama and turn her brothers into swans. Mama had to weave shirts out of nettles for each of them before the allotted time passed to break the spell. So, my uncles – as swans – had to keep Papa away when he came to rescue her. Swans' wings are pretty powerful weapons, and Papa knew they were his princess' brothers, so he didn't dare use his sword. He had to be clever instead.

"The trick was that the moment Mama finished all the shirts and her brothers were human again she was going to turn into a swan – forever. But if she stopped before she was done, her brothers would never be freed."

Daffyd frowned. "This was all a farce, of course. Or maybe an allegory. No one would do that to their own children."

Thony shook his head. "Not at all. I told you last night how Uncle Tommy's right arm stayed a wing. Papa interrupted her before she was quite done."

Daffyd gave him a horrified look. "I missed that. I was too busy thinking about how you have eleven 'middleborn' aunts and uncles."

Thony shrugged again. "The bards made up a song about it: 'The Seven Swans.'"

"Wait, *seven?*" Daffyd demanded. "I must have misunderstood the way you people do things over there. Otherwise – no – he *can't* have had his eldest-born son-and-heir risk being transformed into a swan forever."

This was starting to be seriously awkward for all sorts of reasons that hadn't occurred to Thony before.

I mean, sure, he'd felt kind of sorry for Uncle Tommy with his swan-wing arm, but the one time the man had come visit he'd been so dour and sarcastic and just plain *mean* that everyone had waited with bated breath for him to leave. And Papa had absolutely *forbidden* Thony to even *consider* playing a prank. And Mama had cried for a week after he left.

Everyone talked about how brave Grandpa Dave had been to arrange for the be-swanning... but he'd abdicated in favor of Uncle Joe a few weeks after Mama and Papa's wedding. He and Grandma Marybeth spent their time visiting Aldyrwald and the country where Mama's oldest sister, Marybel, was now Queen. They almost never went home to Silbervale.

"Um, yes?" Thony said.

Daffyd shook his head in disbelief and they rode in silence for the rest of the afternoon.

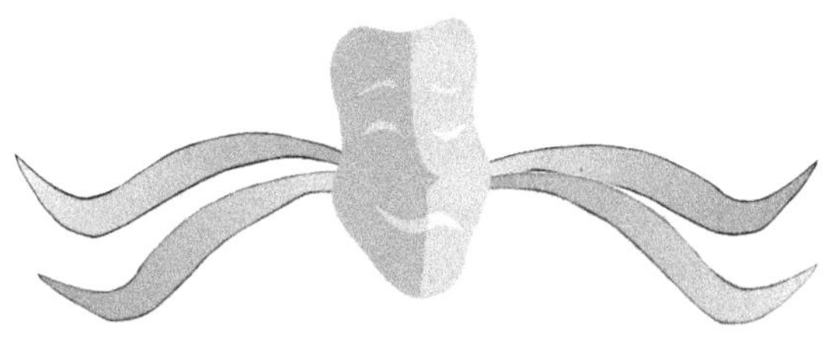

Chapter EIGHT

Getting High

A WEEK OR SO LATER, they were heartily sick of traveling through the mountains.

In Thony's case it was *literally* sick, though the symptoms of altitude sickness never seemed to get much worse than a general feeling of breathlessness and disorientation. It might have helped that they kept going *down* after going *up*.

He'd 'persuaded' Twinklestar not to tattle on him to Daffyd so long as he could mask how he was feeling. There was no hope of hiding it from the unicorn, of course, since Twinklestar could feel Thony's vague nausea and dizziness across their bond, but it was just... darned *embarrassing* for the prince of a *mountain* country to suffer from *altitude sickness*. Even if Mama and Papa's overprotectiveness meant that Thony had spent all his life at one elevation, never going up higher than the height of the castle's tower or down farther than the dungeons.

(Which were not as interesting as they sounded. They hadn't been used in at least a hundred years, and the stories of Great-Grandmother Arabella's cleaning frenzy when she became Queen were apparently not exaggerated.)

The redheaded prince drank as much water as he could manage and never quite reached the barfing stage.

The trip had been both *more* and *less* comfortable than Thony had expected.

Aside from his mild altitude sickness, things were going fairly well. With an extra steed to carry provisions, Puck had added a few things beyond what the boys had raided from the palace kitchens. Namely a tent, extra blankets, a lantern, and some more interesting traveling food than what Thony had thought to 'requisition.'

All of that fit in the extra pair of saddlebags, so Silverfoot's saddle was still available for use and by switching off riders the equines could each get a rest. Twinklestar monitored Silverfoot and Nightbreeze's energy levels and ordered the boys to switch mounts when he felt it was necessary.

So, they were making excellent time.

The tent wasn't terribly large – which was a little awkward – but it kept them warmer at night than they would otherwise have been as the altitude turned Summer's warmth into Fall and then even Winter. Thony had been a little nervous at first about the setup, but they'd shared a room for months on the road, and Daffyd had been a perfect gentleman about it all except for that one time when they were staying with Davril's parents in Dynsfyor. And *hadn't* been sharing a room.

Puck's – or Prince Skiftglow's – directions, however, could have used a little work.

They were *accurate*, it was true, and *detailed*.

They were also just, erm, *wonderfully obscure*, as a certain irritated unicorn colorfully described them. The three of them were, at the time, trotting up and down a canyon and inspecting a series of side-canyons trying to determine which one had a cliff-face that looked 'like Eldest-Princess Reyalla in good mood' on the northwest wall.

It rather said something if the mischievous Fae Prince had managed to irritate a unicorn with Twinklestar's rather abundant sense of humor. On the other hand, Twinklestar had more or less admitted that he was a fairly *young* unicorn and certain comments by the Dark- and Light-elves in Flowerdust had made it clear that Prince Skiftglow had a long and fabled history of irritating other Fae folk.

Daffyd had tried to make a joke of the whole thing, commenting that the hardest part was imagining what his father's mother might actually look like in a good mood. He couldn't remember ever actually seeing her like that.

But all of Puck's instructions were in that vein.

If they weren't hunting for the impressions of royal visages in cliff-faces, they were looking for trees with limbs bent into the shape of certain letters, or red pebbles on a streambed that were set into the shape of a pointing griffin... and it was the griffin's pointing claw that they were to follow next. It was... challenging and rather wearing and seemed more of a test to see if they could – and would – faithfully follow directions than anything else.

On the other hand, Thony wasn't sure how else one *might* provide directions in this labyrinth of canyons and valleys and mountain-passes. A regular map would be useless – some areas had made his compass turn as wildly as the magick one he still had tucked in his wallet had done back when he and Amanita had first met Puck. Presumably there was a great bunch of some magnetic ore nearby them there... which might be useful for Daffyd to know and carry home word of to any interested Pathremiri miners... if he could ever find the place again.

Thony had found himself tempted to take out the little magick compass that Girona Starshine had set to show its holder the direction of their heart's desire – or to guide them on either the safest or the most direct path to get where they were trying to go. He hadn't told Daffyd about the device yet – and had actually felt a little guilty taking it with him without talking to Amanita, even though it had been given specifically and directly to *him,* and she wasn't going anywhere anyways.

In the end, he kept it hidden, slipping his fingers into his beltpouch to touch it occasionally and think about the pair of girls from whom he had received it. The apprentice wizard, Girona, with her aggressively messy hair and her devil-may-care attitude – she was Amanita's 'mirror-twin' on the world of Eyola. And Girona's cousin, the quiet, cheerfully optimistic novice priestess, Midele Featherspray, with her long dark hair and tea-and-milk skin and her warm brown eyes.

They were both middleborn children, but they seemed to be making something of themselves. As had Roger, of course.

Given all these hours with nothing to do but pick their way through these twisty paths and look for Puck's next impossible 'landmark,' Thony had rather too much time to think on such things. Perhaps Daffyd had a point that there was something extremely wasteful about the way the Mountain-Region treated middleborns.

Even Papa had said something about that, the day Thony had left. Something about how they had too many royal children and put too many expectations on them.

What he, Thony, might do about the situation, he had no idea. Or even if he wanted to try.

But he was thinking about it.

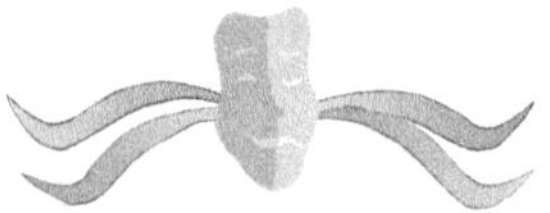

"Okay, *this* one is *absolute nonsense*," Thony's teeth chattered as he held the directions in front of him, his cloak shoved back so he could do so and one glove peeled off so he could turn the fluttering sheets.

They were stopped in one of the higher mountain-passes that they'd been treated to dealing with, and had had to lead the horses through this one. There was a broad saddle between two peaks that each looked more formidable than the young prince wanted to think about – at least Puck's instructions hadn't called for them to climb any of those. Yet.

The wind whistled incessantly past the two humans and three equines, and the trail dropped sharply away twenty feet in either direction. Thony deeply missed the warmth of Twinklestar's body against his legs. Or even Silverfoot's.

Daffyd would keep you warm, Thony, Twinklestar's thought came over, weary but still mischievous.

The Pathremiri prince couldn't hear the unicorn's teasing, but he stepped closer anyways, shielding Thony a bit more from the wind as he looked over the younger boy's shoulder to see what he was reading. After a slight hesitation, he put an arm around Thony's shoulders, drawing his cloak around them both for protection from the wind and confining their combined warmth much as the tent did.

And about as effectively as the tent – they'd both been sleeping in all their layers of clothes for the last few nights.

"What's it say?" Daffyd asked. Standing like this, their heads were close enough together that they didn't need to shout over the whistling wind.

Thony shook his head. "We're in the right place, I know that. We've been *excruciatingly* careful about following his directions. But what are we supposed to do with this?

Be ready to ascend the stairway of clouds.

"And that's the *last line.* Except for some stuff about proper etiquette in Queen Snowmistral's Court. Which I'm not even sure we should trust, because well, *Puck.*"

Daffyd gave a strained chuckle. "Well, he hasn't led us astray yet. And... She's his *Môthir,* right? That makes Her my great-grandmother. I don't think he'd tell us to do something that would put me in bad odor with her."

Thony sighed and leaned close to the older boy as he folded the papers back up. He was so *tired* of being cold. Whatever had possessed him to agree to go hunting down the Court of the Queen of the Snow-Fairies? A Goddess who was known as 'Lady of Blizzards and Gales'?

Though, thankfully, they hadn't had any of those.

Not that *high Summer* should be the time of year for that, either.

"It still doesn't make any *sense*, Daffyd. A stairway of clouds? And there *isn't* one. Is it only here sometimes? Do we have to... *knock* or *ring a bell* or something? Except he doesn't say how to do anything like that. Just *'be ready'*."

Daffyd squeezed his shoulders. "Maybe it does make sense. Snow-Fairies, Mist-Maidens... I've heard they're sometimes called *Cloud*-Maidens, too."

Thony slumped a little. "I'm just so *cold*, Daffyd. And this is higher than we've been. A *lot* higher." He looked guiltily over his shoulder up into the other boy's warm, brown eyes. "I haven't told you before, but I've been having trouble when we go to higher places."

Daffyd frowned, though all Thony could see between hat, hood, and scarves was a small movement around the eyes. "Trouble? What kind of trouble?"

"I think it's altitude sickness," Thony said in a small, miserable voice.

Another movement of Daffyd's face. "But you're mountain-bred."

Thony shrugged slightly. "I don't know how you measure these things. But I'm guessing Aldyrwald's mountains are... lower. A lot lower. Lower even than the Pathremiri Plateau. I started having troubles on the way up from Selavan, but then it seemed to be okay after a few days on the plateau. It's been... coming and going as we go up and down these peaks."

"So... how are you feeling right now?" Daffyd's voice was low and worried.

"Dizzy," Thony admitted. "I'm... not seeing spots, but I... don't think I'm far away from it. Pretty nauseous. I don't think I'm going to throw up..."

He was still downplaying it as best he could, for all he'd decided to tell. No spots – but there were... sparkly swirls of darkness edging in on his vision from the sides. And the real reason he didn't think he was going to throw up was...

"But you didn't eat anything when we stopped for lunch," Daffyd's tone was grim. "And I didn't see if you ate anything for breakfast."

"I didn't," Thony agreed. He tried to take a deeper breath and found himself panting again instead as his body tried to get enough of the air it desperately needed.

"Daffyd," he said, and was dismayed to hear how small his voice had gone. "I'm scared. *Really* scared."

The Pathremiri prince's face was almost invisible behind his scarf, but it sounded like he was sucking in his breath through his teeth. He kept his arm around Thony's shoulders, but moved a little so that he could pull the younger boy in to hold him against his chest.

"We'll fix this, Thony. You'll be okay."

Which would be a great deal more reassuring if only Thony didn't know that Daffyd had no idea how to make that happen.

"I want *Jo,*" he muttered into Daffyd's coat. "I want *Roger.*"

Not that either of them probably knew anything about altitude sickness or making magickal stairways into the clouds appear. But they'd survived their own Quest, hadn't they? And come home covered in unspeakable glories.

And... Roger and Joanna had been solving Thony's problems for him since before he could walk or talk. Mama tended to faint, and... well, for particularly extreme cases, *Papa* tended to faint as well, such as when Prissy was born and the tail... It was probably sort of a miracle that he'd made it through his Quest to win Mama – though, come to think of it, there had never been anything particularly harrowing that was told as his part of the story. Even the witch who had enchanted Mama's brothers hadn't really gotten *involved*.

"They're not here, Thony," Daffyd murmured apologetically. "But I am. I'll take care of you." His head – or rather the pile of scarves and hat and hood that surrounded Daffyd's head – moved. *"Twinklestar and I will take care of you."*

Thony couldn't hear Twinklestar's own comment on that, for some reason, though his unicorn-friend was nudging his shoulder with his nose.

The swirls of sparkly darkness were blacking out most of his vision now, and there was a sort of *buzzing* sound that seemed to go with the swirls.

It was impossible not to start crying, no matter that he was a young *man* now and not a little boy. And that it was too *cold* to cry safely – the tears were freezing on his eyelashes. And that he was already dehydrated, even though he *knew* that drinking water helped with altitude sickness, because their waterskins were low and tasted more leathery than watery at this point and the one taste he'd had this morning had made him gag.

"We'll fix this, Thony, I promise," someone said, and in his dazed, confused state, Thony couldn't be sure who.

But it was a male voice, so...

"Roger?" he asked hopefully... and then the sparkly black swirls won entirely.

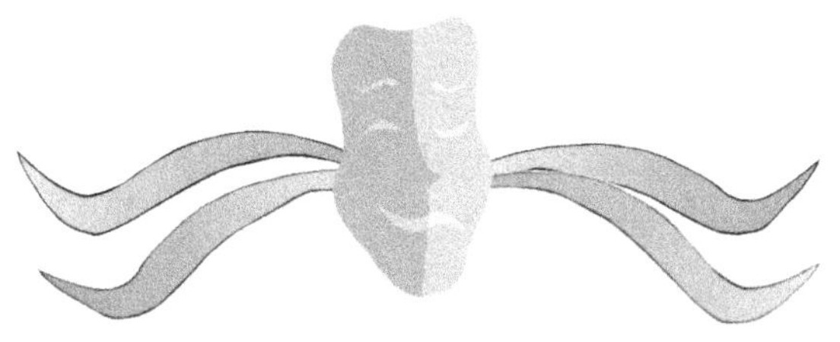

Chapter NINE

Pants

THONY WOKE UP WITH A headache. And surrounded by blinding whiteness on all sides.

His first thought was that the altitude sickness had killed him and this is what Death looked like.

He could breathe just fine now and he didn't feel like he was starving for air and the overpowering fear that he'd been feeling was gone, though he still had a rather overpowering headache. He didn't even remember any nightmares, and he'd been waking up in a cold sweat the last three nights.

On the other hand, all he could see was *WHITE*.

Thony sat up and started discerning variations in the whiteness. He was on a bed. There was what looked like a doorframe off to one side and chests of drawers.

And... a window frame? All he could see out of it was more blank whiteness, so maybe it wasn't a window. A picture-frame? That implied a picture. Of... what?

It was also infernally *quiet*.

If he had died, apparently he hadn't gone to where other people go. Which... was probably pretty, um, illuminating. A blank white space, empty of people and anything to be creative with was sort of Thony's personal definition of...

"Oh, good! You're awake!"

The faint line of the doorframe had opened. Daffyd's relief was as patent in his tone as on his face.

And, of course, that was when Thony realized he was *naked*.

Oh, dear *GODS*.

Maybe this was one of those nightmares he'd been waking up from.

PLEASE let this just be a nightmare.

Thony yelped and scrabbled in the whiteness, his fingers finding a furry softness. He grabbed the furry soft whiteness and dragged it up over himself.

Daffyd's snort of laughter wasn't really all *that* well suppressed. "Dude. You haven't got anything I haven't seen before."

Thony glared at him, feeling like his entire *body* was blushing. "There's such a thing as *privacy,* you know."

The Pathremiri prince didn't go back out the door as Thony had hoped he would. Instead, he folded his arms, leaned back against the doorframe, and grinned more broadly. "I guess I shouldn't mention that I helped the Cloud-Maidens undress you, then."

Thony wasn't sure how he could possibly turn any more red...

"What... why..." He couldn't even form a coherent question.

Daffyd's grin softened into something gentler. And more seasoned with relief.

"Thony. By the time they came for us we were all – you, me, Twinklestar, the horses – halfway to freezing to death. And soaked through. And you'd been unconscious for... a long while." He swallowed hard with remembered fear. "The first thing we had to do was get all our clothes and stuff off so they could pack us in warm, dry things. Well, and get us up to their city where they thicken the air."

That... probably made sense. It also didn't help the fact that Thony was *naked* and had no clue where his clothes might even *be*.

"We're in... a Cloud-Maiden city?" he asked, a little distracted.

Daffyd nodded, enthusiasm chasing away some of that fear in his eyes. "Can't you see it out your window? Oh..." He walked over and looked out. "Bad angle from the bed there. My room is up a level on this tower, and the bed's placed a little differently, so I can see out more easily. And... there's a layer of clouds over us right now. But it's really cool if you look from over here."

He glanced back, to where Thony was still clutching the soft whiteness around himself, and rolled his eyes. "Come on, Thony. Come look."

Thony gave him a dark look... but he *did* kind of want to see... whatever there was to see. Something besides this insane whiteness, hopefully.

He gathered the *(thankfully* **opaque***)* soft whiteness and scootched it around to wrap around his waist. There seemed to be rather a lot of it, but he honestly couldn't tell how *much,* or exactly where it was, so that was kind of unnerving. He wanted to wrap it around his shoulders for modesty's sake – he wasn't *cold* at all anymore, he suddenly realized – but if it wasn't long enough to cover his, um, *knees,* that would *not* be okay.

Hopefully more than less covered, he slipped off the bed and shuffled over to the window that Daffyd was standing at.

The Pathremiri prince was right. The view was *amazing.*

It was... like looking into Mama's basket of carded wool. Piles and piles and *piles* of fluffy whiteness formed a landscape – no, a *cloudscape* – of hills, valleys, cottages, and multistory castles taller than anything Thony could have imagined.

Or... were they taller? The scale was impossible to tell. Distance only made sense in the context of things he could understand the size of after all... and there was a sense that none of what he knew about concepts like *size* and *density* made sense here.

There were people moving around, too, in both the near distance and the far distance. But the ones farther away didn't necessarily seem to be *smaller* in his perception. What might be fluffy sheep gamboled over the hillsides.

And *white* had a hundred – no, a *million* – more shades than Thony could have guessed. Grey and lavender, turquoise and cyan, rose and peach and gold and...

"It's unbelievable, isn't it?" Daffyd draped an arm around his shoulders, and Thony stiffened and pulled away.

"Seriously, Thony?" Daffyd asked. "Do you have any idea what I had to do to get you here?"

Thony looked down. "Um..."

Daffyd reached under his chin and tilted Thony's face up to meet his eyes. His smile was wry. And caring. "You thought I was 'Roger' when you were out of your head. He's your sister's husband who's all but your older brother, isn't he."

It wasn't exactly a question, but Thony made an uncomfortable affirmative sound.

"You relied on *me* to take care of you the way *he* would."

"I guess so..." Thony tried to look away. "I mean, you said yourself I was out of my head."

"It was nice to have someone trust me like that," Daffyd said very quietly. "I wouldn't break that trust for all the worlds beyond the Fairy Wood." He paused. "I wouldn't break that trust to try to get you to take me to *your* world beyond the Fairy Wood."

Thony let his eyes stop flickering everywhere but into Daffyd's. "I know why you suggested that. It didn't have to do with me. It had to do with you escaping from Commander-General Taeryl and the Eldest-Princess."

Daffyd sighed and let go of his chin. "True. Mostly true. In any case, I don't *actually* know that Môthir and Amanita would be able to get Grandmother to send enough troops with me to make it worth your while anyways." He took a step back, and now his smile was... rueful? "And when you collapsed on the mountaintop... I discovered that I'd rather be your big brother than... anything else."

"Oh." Thony couldn't imagine what to say to that.

He'd actually spent the last few days wondering whether maybe that really *was* his best solution. Although it really did just put the whole problem off again, even if *he* was okay with it. He needed an Heir, after all, and that meant a *wife*. And a wife willing and able to have enough children – according to Mountain-Region custom – to prove that the Devinthal family *hadn't* lost the Divine Right of Kings.

Fending off the neighbors' greedy little fingers right *now...*

...was only step one.

But Thony was still only fifteen. He had plenty of time left to figure this out.

"So, um, what about *your* situation?" he ventured.

Daffyd shrugged and looked out the window again. "I'm not going home for awhile. We'll see what turns up."

There was something smug and mysterious about the way he said it, but it was clear the Pathremiri prince would be giving no more details.

"So, we'll keep traveling together?" Thony asked.

Daffyd glanced back and gave him a warm smile. "I'd like that. But I want to stay *here* for awhile first."

"Here?" Thony looked out at that... *colorful whiteness.* It was... interesting, he supposed, but it seemed...

It finally clicked for him.

They were on the *other side of the clouds.* Presumably, if you were a bird, and could fly this high, this was what you would see. Everything – and *everyone?* – was made of clouds.

Thony looked uneasily at the floor beneath his feet. As a mountain-bred boy, he was well aware that *clouds* were entirely insubstantial – you could walk up to a mountain-peak and go *through* a cloud. You'd get pretty wet, and that was about it. You couldn't *build structures* out of clouds and expect to go inside and up the stairs and not fall through the floor.

Assuming you could build out of clouds in the first place.

"Here," Daffyd agreed. "In my *great*-grandmother's Court. To... check out this other part of my heritage."

Oh. That's right.

Cloud-Maidens = Mist-Maidens = Snow-Fairies.

And Daffyd was descended of these beings both from the long-ago days and more recently from Puck. *Prince Skiftglow.* The Queen's son.

And Queen Snowmistral was... also a Goddess.

And Puck had said that She wanted to meet Thony. In *particular.* Which was why he'd come to Pathremir.

"Ready to meet our hosts, Thony?"

The redheaded prince squared his shoulders.

"I am. As soon as we can find me some pants."

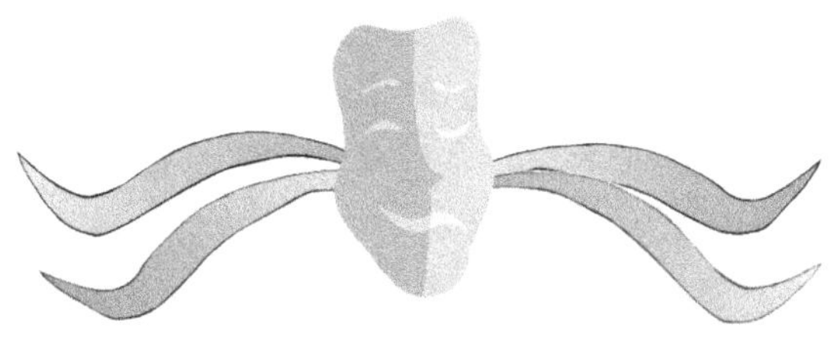

Chapter TEN

Her Cheerful Majesty

IT TURNED OUT THONY'S CLOTHES had been in one of those chests of drawers around his room. Everything had been cleaned, folded, and put away. Daffyd had helped him get out a set of the formal outfits that he'd been collecting along the way – in Dysacha, Dysnfyor, and in the Queen's City – and then stepped outside so that Thony could dress in peace.

And, um, take care of a few other little personal things. *(There was a washroom attached to the bedchamber, to his **literal** relief.)*

He'd also pointed out a flask of water with a cup and some *(white)* food sitting atop a different chest of drawers. The food seemed to taste sort of like bread... or fruit... or... Thony gave up trying to identify it. Between sips of the water and bites of the food, his headache cleared up quickly.

When Thony came out of the room, he gave Daffyd a hug and thanked him for taking care of him. He'd been... rather less than gracious when he'd woken up, after all.

Daffyd was understanding, and led him through corridors that... didn't seem to exactly have flat walls. They bulged a bit, rather like unfinished stone... but felt soft and squishy to the touch. It was pretty weird. Cool, but weird.

At least his vision was beginning to adjust, and – although everything still looked washed-out – Thony could distinguish colors and shading enough to be able to tell the floor apart from the walls and so on.

And people.

The people were... just as weird close-up as he'd had the impression that they were from far off. Some of them looked like normal people, but some seemed to be as intangible as... mist, and appeared somewhat distressed by the drafts of air that his and Daffyd's passage were causing.

Some of the insubstantial ones were very tall and almost see-through – which led Thony to try to figure out exactly what he meant by even *thinking* the words 'almost see-through.'

Most of the 'normal' ones seemed short.

Some of them were *quite* short. Thony saw a mother and her daughters – each carrying a baby or herding a toddler of her own – and none of their heads came up above his waist.

There was a preponderance of females. Which he supposed made sense, given that they *were* called Mist- or Cloud-*Maidens*, after all. He wondered if there really were more females, and if that had been true in the ancient Land of Mists, when they had inter-bred with humans.

And how the *dragons,* who had supposedly *also* inter-bred with humans *(speaking of mind-boggling),* fit into everything.

The people got *stranger* to Thony's eyes as the number of passersby increased.

One woman appeared to be entirely unclothed – which would normally have had Thony blushing and turning away – but she *(or maybe that should be 'she')* looked more like a snowstorm contained within the shape of a human form than a flesh-and-blood person. The swirling snow that seemed to fill her up reminded Thony of the paperweights a traveling merchant had brought to Aldyrwald a few years ago: baubles of glass with a little scene set inside that looked like they were having a blizzard if you turned them upside-down or shook them.

(He'd collected the insides of several of the fragile things and determined it was no more than a trick. The 'snow' was little chips of what seemed to be porcelain, and the whole thing was filled with a light, clear oil. They made an unGodly mess when they broke.)*

"That's Suzarrah Snowflake," Daffyd whispered, pulling him along quickly. "Don't look at her too hard or she'll notice you."

"And that would be... bad?" Thony asked, trying to tear his eyes away from the fascinating creature.

"Yes." Daffyd didn't explain, but he sounded serious, and Thony sighed and looked where they were headed next.

Which was very much worth another look.

This must be Queen Snowmistral's throne-room.

It was brighter and airier than the dark and dingy *(until lit by the King and Queen's own Presence)* throne-room of Selavan. More tasteful than the ornately overdone throne-room in Dysacha. And... well, Thony realized he'd never seen Queen Namarina's throne-room during the week or so he'd been in Pathremir's Queen-City. It was more regal than Papa's, anyways.

There seemed to be few architectural constraints when building with clouds – the ceiling floated incredibly high above them, the central chamber braced with must be *literal* flying buttresses. Windows peeked out to allow light to fill the airy space and patches of brilliantly blue sky to peer in. The floor appeared to be as smooth as clear glass – clouds billowed beneath it in a pulsating swirl that Thony found slightly nauseating – but underfoot it had the texture of a soft carpet.

** Note to readers – **modern** snow globes contain bits of plastic snow, and the liquid is glycerol and **anti-freeze** in water – which is **toxic.** The earliest snow globes were made like the ones Thony explored.*

Queen Snowmistral Herself lounged on a wide-seated throne at the end of the hall, surrounded by ladies nearly as beautiful as She was.

(And possibly some guys, too. Thony didn't really notice.)

The Queen had a cloud of black hair that seemed to rise around Her, and skin the color of the setting sun. A crown of what looked like flying sparks of fire danced around Her head and She seemed to have rainbows for jewelry. Her gossamer gown shaded from shimmery white at Her shoulders to starry black at its full and rippling hem, and Her full sleeves were slashed to show glimpses of Her rounded arms as She gestured animatedly to emphasize what She was telling Her ladies. Her feet seemed to be tucked up underneath Her on Her royal seat, and She was leaning far to Her left, half-draped over the arm of Her throne as She engaged in the discussion.

(The 'setting sun' thing wasn't really a great description, but Thony was kind of giving up on those for the time being. This place was sort of made to be poetic about. In this case, however, Her skin was the sort of peachy-golden color that the clouds get sometimes. But more on the golden side, like She was tanned, rather than peachier and looking like She was sunburned. Or blushing.)

Her ladies also all had cloudy hair in a variety of different shades ranging from grey *(though that one didn't look old)* and white *(this one did)* through a sunshiney-golden and other colors he'd never seen on people's heads before *(except right after his prank in Selavan)*, like purple and a peachy-rosy shade.

The white-haired one *(who seemed to have some age to her)* noted the boys' approach and tapped her Queen's leg to draw Her attention.

"Grandson!" Queen Snowmistral exclaimed delightedly. "Thank you, Eurosa. Bora, we'll have to finish this discussion later."

She uncurled and came down from Her throne and the stepped dais it was set upon with a couple of bounds. Thony had expected Her to float, but it was quickly clear that floating was far too dignified for this Being.

When he tried to bow, the Queen/Goddess pulled him up into a hug that was... nice, but a bit embarrassing, given how very, um, *low* her neckline was, and how, um, *much* she had to put in it.

Daffyd got an energetic hug of his own, and then the Queen had an arm around each of them and proceeded to give them both a guided tour of her domain.

Thony found it incredibly hard to think of this beaming, energetic woman as a *Goddess*. She seemed intent on being just Daffyd's great-grandmother. *(If altogether too young-looking to pull it off properly... not that Daffyd seemed bothered, but then Queen Namarina was rather younger – and younger-looking – than any of Thony's remaining grandparents also.)*

"You'll have to tell me all about what happened in Flowerdust," Queen Snowmistral informed the boys as she guided them through some of those hills and valleys *(and yes, some of those creases really were **streams** as Thony had half-guessed from his tower-room... but it was some sort of misty breeze that flowed, not water... although the Queen said it would make him quite nearly as wet. And there were some kind of fish...)*

"I thought you... I mean You, knew all that kind of stuff," Thony managed to ask.

He'd been asking more questions than Daffyd on this whirlwind *(not literally... quite)* tour of the Cloud-Country. He wasn't sure if that was because his friend *(his... new substitute older brother? That still seemed weird...)* had already had this tour, or because he was just a quieter sort.

Daffyd had been fairly quiet around the Pathremiri women *(which had been, like **all the time** that Thony had known him up until their escape)*. And he'd been reasonably quiet – except for a few loooong conversations – while they were following Puck's directions. Though there had been a lot of huffing and puffing and single-filing it and persuading Nightbreeze and Silverfoot to make it through narrow cuts or along narrow ledges... and they'd usually been pretty exhausted after the first couple of days to do more than cook and go to bed.

Or at least Thony had, as the cumulative effect of the altitude changes had caught up with him.

But a quick look at Daffyd's face *now,* made it clear that he was absolutely delighted to be here, not holding his tongue out of fear or prudence or whatever.

The Queen shrugged. "Oh, I know the general ideas, but I can't really access that area terribly well, though I have some occasional contact in the Winter. In the Spring – I have to rely on reports from my brother- and sister-winds."

She rolled eyes that Thony had decided were the most *beautiful* grey eyes he had ever seen. "And let me tell *you.* Plains-land winds either have the driest sense of humor you've ever seen – and you can never quite tell if they're just ribbing you – or else they have the prickliest tempers and any little thing will set off a string of tornadoes.

"I'd like to hear *your* version – I heard you strengthened Puck with pranks. I want to hear *all* about the *pranks!*"

Her grin was infectious as she led them into a pasture-type area where Twinklestar was keeping an eye on the two horses.

Thony was pleased to find someone adultish – other than Puck – who really seemed to appreciate the idea of pranks. Puck must have gotten that from his mother.

But the redheaded prince was immediately distracted by seeing Twinklestar. Thony didn't know how long he'd been recovering from the altitude sickness – neither Daffyd nor the Queen had mentioned it – but it *felt* like it had been *ages* since he'd touched his unicorn-friend.

And Twinklestar clearly felt the same. He buried his nose in Thony's chest, nuzzling, before he let the boy hug him around the neck for awhile.

Missed you, the unicorn said simply.

"I'd say I missed you, too, but I think I was asleep or unconscious or something."

The Queen was Healing you. Most of that was sleeping. I was 'listening' in when you came close enough to alertness that I could use your ears. And Daffyd came down and gave me details.

He nuzzled Thony's hair, and the boy laughed and pushed his unicorn's face away. "Don't you dare get slime in my hair again!" The prince hugged him close again, and said very quietly, "I love you."

*I love you, too. Though it will be nice when we can find some proper ladies for me **and** you. I miss Chillabiaen. And Rainsparkle.*

"I thought Nightbreeze was a lady-horse."

There was a hesitation, as if Twinklestar was trying to tone down his tendency to be blunt and snarky. *Nightbreeze is very beautiful... but she's just a **horse**. A very **smart** horse, but...there's not a lot there to talk to.*

That seemed fair. Thony's own experience with various equines had confirmed that unicorns were something entirely different. *And Chillabiaen? Isn't she 'just a horse?'*

Twinklestar actually neighed in a horsey laugh over that. *Um, Thony, you **saw** the teeth of the **hrulga** stallion that Lady Opalsinger lent Stillheart. I **know** you did.*

Thony felt his eyes go very wide. *Chillabiaen is... one of **those?** But she was tiny when we were in Fairyland – and she had... wings.*

Twinklestar gave a horsey shrug – the skin bunched up and then the crinkle moved like a wave across a good section of his body as he shook his head vigorously. *And the other **hrulgin** would look like that when they are of a size to visit the Fairy Queen's Court as well.*

"Oh..." Thony didn't so much shrug as shiver. "I never saw her teeth..."

She is very polite. She is also not a 'horse.'

"Oh..." Thony said again. Puck seemed even braver now.

The Queen is watching us.

Thony looked up to see Queen Snowmistral standing a little ways away, a small smile on her face. She brightened when he met her eye, then turned her gaze to check on Daffyd, who was checking on Nightbreeze. And Silverfoot.

Thony immediately felt guilty...

Don't. He is pleased to be useful and important, as he was not allowed to be in Pathremir. And the Cloud-Maidens groomed us all very thoroughly when they brought us up here, and there is nothing in this place to make us dirty or snag our manes and tails. No dust to roll in...

Twinklestar heaved a great sigh, *But there's also no stones to catch in hooves. Though I would need my hooves trimmed very frequently if we stayed here long.*

"I don't think we plan to..." Thony shrugged. "Though I'm not sure *how* long. Daffyd wants to get to know his kin. And... I have nowhere I need to be, particularly." It felt a little weird, saying that. "Let me know when you need a hoof trim, okay? Or anything else."

I will. And it's a little boring with just the horses, but after all the traveling and mountain-climbing, it's nice to rest for awhile. This place is very easy on the feet.

Thony looked down at the... hill made of clouds. "It's weird. It's soft to walk on, but it doesn't mess with your balance. And... that's not really *grass*, is it? Are you getting enough to eat?"

Twinklestar snorted a little. *It is most excellent eating.* **Too excellent,** *for all that I had to bully the horses into even trying it at first. I need to chase them around to keep them from eating too much and getting fat or upsetting their stomachs.*

"Are they at risk of colic?" Thony asked with alarm.

There had been one Spring back home when the horses were given too much time on the lush new growth and had become very ill. A couple, he remembered sadly, had even had to be put down because of the painful gases developing in their abdomens, despite extreme measures that the local animal physick had taken to save them.

Horses couldn't burp... which had been the first time Thony had ever thought about that bodily function as a life-saving device. He'd been too sad to pull any pranks for a long time after that...

Though eventually the idea of burping and noxious gases had fueled his work with beans and broccoli in the kitchens of the Raven HQ in Flowerdust. So, at least those horses' deaths hadn't been entirely in vain.

I'm taking care of them, Thony.

The redheaded prince nodded. If anyone should be able to prevent such a tragedy, it would be Twinklestar. "I would like to go for a ride with you, but... I should probably get back to the Queen. She surely can't wait around all day for us."

Come back tomorrow, then.

Thony gave his unicorn-friend another hug, and made his way back to Queen Snowmistral. Daffyd had beat him there and was talking quietly to his great-grandmother.

"You and Twinklestar are adorable together," the Queen said as they both turned to look at Thony. "I think you may be the very first boy ever Chosen by a unicorn... but somehow I don't think you'll be the last."

Thony gave her an uncertain look. Was that supposed to be a *good* thing?

"You have questions, Thony," the Queen said as they all began to walk away. "Ask me."

"Oh, um..." He had about three hundred *million* questions. Where to start? "Why is Puck's hair so pale if he's your son? Yours is super-black. And... um, should we be calling him 'Prince Skiftglow' now?"

Daffyd rubbed a hand over his face as he shook his head, but Thony could see the smile under it. A weird sort of *'I can't believe he said that'* kind of deal.

"She said to *ask,*" Thony told his friend a little offendedly.

"And I wanted him to ask," Queen Snowmistral laughed and draped her arms around both of their shoulders again. She was just taller-enough to make it comfortable for all of them... it made

Thony feel like a little boy again, but in the good way. The 'you are protected and loved and appreciated' way, not the 'you may not do anything unless we let you' way.

Puck was really lucky.

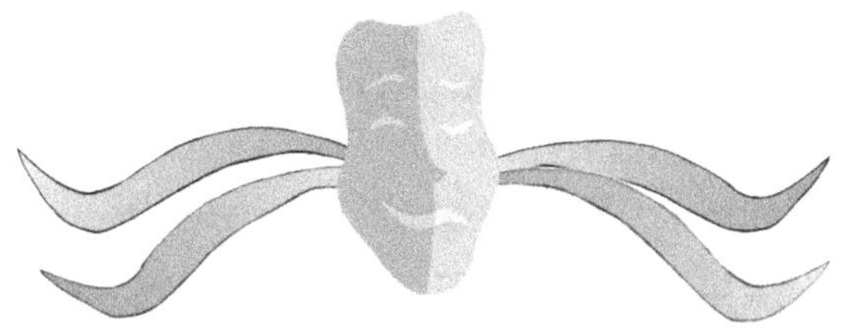

Chapter ELEVEN

Just a Peek

Q UEEN SNOWMISTRAL'S COURT WAS A fun place to be.

The Queen herself clearly appreciated having them there, and her attendants and courtiers seemed pleased as well. The two boys never lacked for people to play a game, discuss philosophy or politics, or twirl around the floor in one of the balls that filled many of the evenings. The food was tremendous – if never really identifiable to Thony – and they were slowly accumulating a supply of Cloud-Court clothing.

Daffyd was getting to know his cousins – some of whom were thousands of years older than him, but they seemed as young as he.

Thony and Daffyd went for rides daily, often taking one – or more, if they cared to ride pillion – of the Cloud-Maidens or -Men along as well. He and Twinklestar were seeing a great deal of each other, and in a more relaxed atmosphere than they'd had so far.

There were no deep and dark undercurrents as there had been in the other Courts that Thony had visited. Everything seemed – and *was* – light and airy and happy.

The place reminded Thony of *home* more than any of the *human* Courts that he had visited. After all, despite the Issues with the Neighbors, King Bill's Court was a pleasant place to be. The biggest drama usually came when one of Thony's pranks was outed, and that didn't last terribly long.

The redheaded young prince found himself both very happy and fighting bouts of incredible homesickness.

And... actually kind of bored.

It seemed *weird* to be bored and having fun at the same time, though he'd had a different flavor of the same dessert at King Mithral and Queen Lochea's Court in Selavan. There was a lot *going on* and always something to *do*... but not a lot of *reason* to be doing any of it.

Which was kind of the same deal that Thony had had at home, leaving aside the lessons Mama and Papa had required and which he'd long since out-grown.

Daffyd, however, was clearly not ready to leave.

So, Thony found other things to amuse himself. He located the Court Library and he sought out someone to teach him more swordsmanship and bow-work.

*(Archery proved to be a wash. Beings who were essentially One with the air itself didn't need practice to make their arrows go where they wished, and Thony couldn't actually work with their kinds of bows – which were more decorative than functional. Trying to use his **own** bow and arrows resulted in an unintentional game of 'fetch' for his new Cloud-people friends, since his arrows slid right through whatever enchantment was holding him and Daffyd from falling to the ground unimaginably far below.)*

It helped, but not really enough.

When Queen Snowmistral informed the boys that she'd be busy for a few days, even Daffyd was starting to seem a little restless.

"You'll need to stay out of the throne-room," the Queen told them. "And... actually, out of the main parts of the castle wouldn't be a bad idea either. Your tower will connect you to the kitchens and pastures and the library – all the places you usually go."

'Will connect' indeed. A random comment from Thony about how long the walk was to the kitchens had occasioned a re-design that ended up with the tower-top that had their bedrooms in it being floated over, right next to the kitchens.

'Because growing boys need to eat when they're hungry!' the Queen had said with a cheery wink... It had taken them an extra hour to figure out how to *find* their bedrooms again, but the nearness to the kitchens had mollified even Daffyd.

(What the servants thought about this sort of thing, Thony wouldn't hazard a guess.)

Apparently, there were advantages to building castles in the sky.

And out of clouds.

Right now, however, Daffyd was furrowing his brow and a shade of that anxiety that Thony hadn't even realized had previously shadowed his friend's every expression was back.

"Have I done something wrong, Grandmother?" the Pathremiri prince asked hesitantly. And then, with an even more hesitant glance at Thony. "Or, um, *we?*"

Thony rolled his eyes.

Queen Snowmistral shook her head. "Not at all, love. I just have some... special guests stopping in. And some of them are... a little touchy. I won't have most of my Cloud-Maidens present either. They are long-lived, but still mortal and... it's just safer to have mortals out of the way of these guests."

She ruffled Thony's hair and gave Daffyd a quick, one-armed hug. "I'll miss you, but... this is our annual meeting."

Daffyd nodded, but his posture still lacked a certain starch. It bothered Thony to see how much his friend depended on such external validation.

Those 'touchy guests' had arrived yesterday, and the castle was all a-flutter with excitement.

Only the Queen's six ladies – the ones who sat beside her throne when she was there – were allowed into the throne-hall. A skeleton staff provided service to the rest of the main castle areas, including the guest-rooms; word in the kitchens was that those servers had drawn the short straws.

Twinklestar had at first been in raptures, as *other* magickal equines began to fill his pastures... But all too soon he was telling Thony that he was taking Nightbreeze and Silverfoot and finding safer places. 'Don't find us, we'll find you' had been the implication.

"Let's go take a look at these creatures that scared Twinklestar off," Thony suggested after the two of them had spent all day staring out of Daffyd's bedroom window *(his room was the higher one and thus had the better view, and his window was wider)* hoping to catch a glimpse of the visitors coming or going. They'd been chased out of the kitchens by the harried cooks, and their usual friends all seemed to either be busy or have mysteriously evaporated *(perhaps literally... Cloud-folk, after all...).*

The Pathremiri prince gave him an incredulous look. "Twinklestar told you they were too dangerous for *him* to be around. What makes you think it would be a good idea for *us* to be there?"

Thony turned his back to the view and leaned his elbows on the broad windowsill. "He's probably just looking out for *our* horses," he said, ignoring his own words of a moment earlier. "He'd probably be fine with them himself."

"Uh-*hunh*. And *that's* why he's taking them so far off that he won't even be able to *hear* you."

"Come on, Daffyd. I'm not suggesting we try to *groom* them or something. Just go close enough to get a *peek* and see what they are." He watched the older boy's dubious expression and decided to throw out a finishing stroke. "Nevermind. I know this isn't really your sort of thing. I'll go myself. It's just... if Amanita were here, I'd've asked her."

It was... kind of unfair.

He *knew* that Daffyd had always felt he had to be the Good Kid while Amanita could do whatever the hell she wanted and get away with it. Not with their parents, Thony had sussed out – their mother and father treated them pretty equally – nor even with their grandmother, Queen Namarina. But around everyone *else* in Pathremir...

He also knew that the caution and self-restraint had become a core part of Daffyd's personality. And if a part of the young man yearned for adventure – well, it was usually a pretty well-controlled and suppressed part.

If Dell and the other street-kids hadn't intercepted them on the way out of the Queen's City and Daffyd hadn't been confused and distracted... Thony was almost entirely certain the other boy would have gone back.

But after that long and emotionally trying afternoon conversation – and the kiss that had put Daffyd so out of sorts – and then being *escorted* to where the horses were waiting for them...

Thony wasn't sure if it had become a point of *pride* for Daffyd not to turn back, or what. The Pathremiri prince had been *steadier* on the journey to find Queen Snowmistral's Court than Thony would have expected as well.

Perhaps it was simply that Daffyd tended to dither until he was past the point of no return on a decision.

Whatever, the reference to his 'hellion of a sister' had Daffyd's brown eyes flashing. *He* knew when he was being manipulated, and it clearly annoyed him that he was helpless prey to such a comment.

"Fine. Let's go."

Daffyd pulled himself back from the window and started for the door.

Thony hung back, watching his friend until the older prince irritably snatched the door open and looked back to narrow his eyes when he saw Thony hadn't moved.

"This was *your* idea, Thony. Aren't you coming?"

"We don't have to do this Daffyd," Thony made his tone as sincere as he could. "Really. It was just an idea. I'm just bored." He paused. "I should probably just go to the Library or something. That's not off-limits, is it?"

Daffyd glared at him. "I *grew up* with Amanita, Thony. I'm well aware that if I let you go off 'to the Library'," and he made air-quotes when he said it, "you'll be going off to do the stupid thing anyways. On your lonesome. And then *I'll*–"

Daffyd clamped his teeth together on the rest of what he was going to say, but he didn't have to say anything. *He'd* get blamed for letting Thony run off. As he must've done when Amanita did.

Again, probably not by his parents or his grandmother... *(Or at least the **one** grandmother...)*

Thony winced internally, but it was kind of too late to back off. If he tried, Daffyd wouldn't believe him. And the longer he tried to delay their departure, the more upset Daffyd would likely get.

At least, that was how it had worked with Prissy.

He heaved himself off of his elbows and out of the windowsill. "All right."

And so, they went.

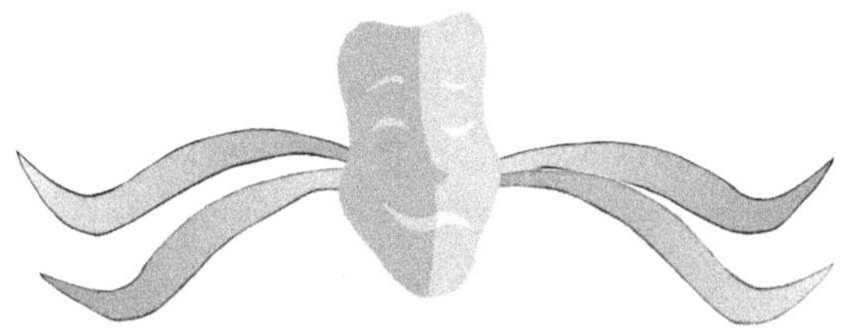

Chapter TWELVE

Here, Horsie, Horsie…

"This… was a really stupid idea." Daffyd muttered for about the twenty-third time.

"*Sshhh!*" Thony whispered back. *"They'll hear us."*

The creatures grazing in the meadow resembled horses the way Lady Opalsinger – the princess of the Dark-elves – resembled a human.

There were several sets of them, actually. Beautiful of form, some with golden coats and manes and tails of red or orange, some the other way around. In their presumed privacy, they nibbled peacefully at the not-grass on the cloud-hill.

If it weren't for the fact that most of their manes seemed to actually be *made of flames,* and their hooves *glowed* like they were used to *treading on stars…* well, even then they wouldn't have looked like normal horses.

There were a handful of chariots parked around the pasture. Presumably each set of horses belonged to one of the chariots. Most of them were free – but one set looked fairly miserable, their yokes still attached and limiting where they could graze.

Thony felt sorry for that set. They seemed to have eaten all the cloud-grass within their reach and be fruitlessly hunting around for more. To make matters worse, the horses from the *other* chariots were clearly *courting* each other.

The young prince had spent one Spring gazing out the windows of his schoolroom and watching the breeding herds of horses that the herdsmen had brought in from the highest pastures *(Master Eswith had not really been on board with that kind of education and Thony had gotten extra assignments – though that had been when the assignments were more useful than pointless Court etiquette).* He'd learned by observation what a stallion might do to catch the interest of a mare – it wasn't, after all, all that different from what he saw the knights and squires doing to catch the eye of one or another of Mama's ladies-in-waiting.

Daffyd was tugging on his sleeve, trying to get him to sneak off with him. They'd had their *peek,* the older boy's eyes seemed to say. Now it was time to go back.

Thony nodded and began to crawl away after his friend. The plan was to keep low to avoid notice, just the way they'd come in. It was a good thing the colorless cloud-grass didn't leave stains and the colorless dirt didn't either, given that they hadn't anticipated needing to do any crawling and so hadn't bothered to change into their old clothes. Although the Cloud-Court clothes they were wearing probably helped them blend in to the colorless hillside rather better... and covered their too-vivid skins up as well.

But the predicament of those tethered horses ate at his heart.

Their master must be terribly cruel.

He hadn't *consciously* decided to stop following Daffyd when he realized he was getting *closer* to the little knots of horses rather than farther away.

It was... probably not the brightest idea.

But it *bugged* Thony that those horses were being mistreated. Weird and dangerous-looking though they were.

And as long as he was over here anyways...

How hard could it be to sneak over there and unhitch them? Then they could get at more of the pasture, or go down to drink from the not-quite-a-stream *(Twinklestar had assured him that whatever was flowing slaked your thirst pretty well).*

Actually, he'd just be doing the owner of those horses a *favor,* if you thought about it right. They'd obviously been in a hurry and hadn't had time to properly see to their beasts. Maybe he'd been late to this mysterious meeting that Queen Snowmistral was hosting.

Thony inched his way forwards, being careful not to startle any of the *other* terrifying-looking horses in the pasture. They were more of a mixed bunch than he had realized from farther off.

Closest to the edge were a set of the flaming red-gold horses that Thony had seen while he was sneaking around with Daffyd. A two-wheeled chariot – plain in lines, but decorated with what seemed to be ivy – rested on its draught pole, looking a bit sad and slumped over.

A set of seven grazed together, each one shimmering out one of the colors of the rainbow from among the sparks of flame that seemed to compose their manes and tails. The giant, twelve-wheeled chariot waiting nearby them almost seemed to be an entire, gold-trimmed building – a bit overdone and impractical to Thony's way of thinking, but presumably the owner had *reasons.*

A much more utilitarian chariot – more of a cart, really – was near a pair of horses that seemed to *flicker* and suddenly be elsewhere. They seemed to be playing a game of tag, which is totally what Thony would have done if *he* could move that fast.

Five other horses whose hides were of a sky-like turquoise blue, a very soft white, a pearly white, an overly vivid red, and utter black clumped together. They had rather minimalistic saddles and no chariot whatsoever nearby them.

And then there was a particularly beautiful white mare with the longest, silkiest-looking mane and tail of any horse that Thony had ever seen. She was almost luminous and it was hard to see why she might belong in this assemblage.

Nevermind. Not his problem.

Thony had one task and he was going to get that done – flaming horses or not – and then get out of here before he discovered that any of *these* horses were close kin to the *hrulgin* that the members of the Fairy Queen's Court all seemed to ride.

Though it *was* kind of weird that even the unbound horses were all staying in their little groupings. In Thony's experience, horses were very social animals and tended to enjoy meeting other horses.

Oh, well. It sort of made it easier to get across the meadow of not-grass to where the...

Oh.

Hmmn.

That was weird.

Where he could *swear*, he had seen *one* golden chariot, and a bunch of horses tethered to it, there was now... An entire *fleet* of chariots, all that shimmering gold. And there was a whole herd of crazy red-gold *cows* instead of horses at all.

Cattle, he supposed he should call them, since he had no idea if they were boy cows or girl cows. They all seemed to have horns, though.

And they were all still attached to the chariots... er... chariot, singular. Hunh?

Thony frowned, trying to make sense of it all.

Well, whatever.

Cattle or horses, they didn't deserve to be left all tied up like that. Though... those horns made the job seem more dangero– er, *complicated*...

He turned to look back behind him, to see if Daffyd had realized Thony wasn't with him yet.

Yep, there was the Pathremiri prince, standing a few cloud-hills over and looking like he was trying to figure out how to get Thony's attention without waving something around that might spook the horses. And cattle.

The luminous white mare seemed to be watching Thony solemnly.

Did she know something he didn't?

Well, no help for it now.

He turned around again and... it was still *one* golden chariot, but now there were horses attached to it again. Well, no horns.

Thony had been riding since he was five and knew better than to approach strange horses – well, *any* horses, really, from the rear. So, he made his way to the front of the traces and stopped there, some ten feet forwards of the lead pair, waiting for them to notice him so that he could try to make friends enough to get in and unhitch them from the draught-pole.

The horses ignored him, nosing around for more of the not-grass.

Thony waited, patiently. Patience was an extremely important skill for any prankster, so it was one of his more-developed character traits. If need be, he could out-wait the Gods. *(Well, and he **had,** on more than one occasion, lying in wait for Jo or Prissy to return from some God-Thing or other.)*

Eventually, one of the beautiful red-gold creatures deigned to look at him. She looked bored, actually. He could have sworn that a slight spark of interest lit her eye as she looked at him and that she did... *something* to get her partner's attention.

With both of the lead horses looking at him, Thony approached carefully. He'd had horse-etiquette drilled into him since he was small as well, and he'd been heading down to see a herd of horses. So, his pockets bulged with apples and cubes of sugar. Daffyd had objected to this, when they were heading down, but Thony had known it was important, so he hadn't listened.

Carefully, he offered an apple on a flat hand to each of them and ignored what seemed to be *actual* sparks of flame flickering down around him. It was probably just 'fireflies' – which was what Queen Snowmistral had called the little glowing specks that formed her crown.

He got the usual snuffly *whuffles* before two sets of great teeth crunched in.

There was a... sudden straightening up and *attention* from all the horses behind this first pair at that very distinctive sound. Thony almost laughed as it became clear that they *all* wanted an apple.

"I don't know if I have enough for *everyone,*" he said, offering ear- and cheek-scratches to the pair he'd already fed. "I wasn't anticipating there being so many of you. But, oh! You *are* beauties, aren't you? I suppose I can go raid the kitchens once I have you all freed, assuming that Daffyd doesn't tattle on me."

Talking in a soothing tone was part of convincing horses to like you, so he kept on in the same vein as he made his way back to where the traces for the first pair connected to the draught-pole.

The next pair were looking at him hungrily, so he pulled out another pair of apples and offered those to them. He didn't *think* they could press far enough forwards in their traces to reach his hands while he was working on freeing the first pair, but – better safe than sorry, right?

"Thony!"

He heard a strangled whisper from up ahead of him and realized that Daffyd had apparently snuck across the field as well and climbed up into the golden chariot. The frantic looks the older prince was giving the area around him suggested that he was terrified of all the unusual horses.

Thony smiled up at him. "Hi, Daffyd. Someone forgot to undo the traces to let these beauties graze properly and get a drink."

"Thony – this isn't safe!"

"It won't take but a few minutes," Thony said, returning his attention to the straps. This was a very unfamiliar configuration for buckles... and the draught-pole was flatter and wider than he would have expected. Not that he knew a lot about the traces on chariots. Or even carriages. "It's not right to leave them tied up like this."

*"Thony, will you just **look around you?!**"*

With a certain exasperation, the redheaded prince looked up again. He was right between the first pair, and their shoulders were higher than his head. But he glanced over his shoulder...

...and then, with some dismay, *under* the bellies of the horses he was intending to free.

Apparently, that sound of a crunching apple had attracted the attention of... rather more than just the horses who were still strapped to the chariot.

In fact, it was possible that *every* horse in the entire *pasture-area* had decided to come see if there were apples for *them*.

The ones Thony was in between stomped a bit, clearly uncomfortable with how they were being crowded. Horses like company, but like any creature that was prey to others, they preferred to have the freedom to move in a crowd. And Thony's feet were entirely too close to *their* feet.

And now the rest of the attached horses were stomping unhappily, too.

And the field beyond was... packed rather closely...

He looked up at Daffyd's increasingly nervous face as he regarded the redheaded prince from the golden chariot, and abruptly decided he'd rather be up *there* than down *here*. And the only way up to where the Pathremiri prince stood was... to somehow walk along the wide, flat draught-pole between the agitated horses.

Who were *definitely* throwing off sparks now.

At least, with so many of them shifting more or less in place, the pole itself was staying relatively steady.

Thony had always felt he had pretty good balance...

Apparently now was the time to test it.

"Help me out, friends, please," he muttered to the lead horses and the secondary ones. "I can't bring *any* of you more apples if I can't get out of here safely myself."

Carefully, Thony hoisted himself up onto the 'wide' beam of the draught-pole. It no longer looked like any such thing, now that he was having to balance on it.

Firmly, the redheaded prince reminded himself that he had been walking along the top-rails of the 'Desert Pasture' back home for years. And rickety as *that* thing always seemed, he should be used to something swaying under his feet...

Daffyd did not look *less* terrified as Thony made his way, step by careful step closer. The redheaded prince decided to focus on his friend, rather than the avid gazes of all those fearsome horses that *had* been scattered all over the hillsides.

The chariot seemed a million miles away... How many horses could there possibly *be* hooked up to it?

It didn't help that Thony had to stop and parcel out goodies to each pair that he passed. And that the unattached horses pressed closer in every time he did. They had definitely figured out where the treats were coming from. There was a sense of discontent when he switched from apples to sugar, followed by a sense of mollification.

And then, of course, Thony's pockets were empty.

He looked helplessly at the next pair of expectant gazes, and then up at Daffyd.

"I'm sorry?" he told the horses. "I don't have any more apples or sugar."

They glared at him, clearly dissatisfied with his answer.

"If... if you help me get out of here safely, I'll bring back more, though."

If he hadn't spent the last several months communicating with Twinklestar, it might have seemed pretty weird to try to negotiate with a horse. *Horses.*

Thony had *no real idea* if these were *equine beings* that could be reasoned with, along the order of unicorns or *hrulgin,* or just regular horses.

Okay, they were *clearly* not 'regular horses.' But that didn't give him a clue as to how smart they were.

If only Twinklestar was here to interpret...

Of course, if Twinklestar was here, he'd probably have warned Thony off of this stupid idea.

Which Daffyd *had* tried to do.

Maybe Twinklestar wouldn't have been any more effective. Thony knew he was pretty stubborn at times, and he really *hated* to see an animal being mistreated. *(He still felt guilty that they hadn't been able to do more about that sleazy horse-dealer back in Flowerdust.)*

But at least Twinklestar could've translated what Thony was saying into horse-language.

The horses in the traces seemed to be communicating with each other somehow. Thony wasn't sure *what* they were saying to each other, but he'd been around horses long enough to figure out that that they *were* saying something to each other via body language.

He looked up to meet Daffyd's eyes. The older prince stretched out a hand, though they were still much too far apart to try to reach each other.

Thony tried to give his friend a confident smile back. Even if he didn't feel all that confident on the inside, it wouldn't do a great deal to show it right now.

There was always a better time to doubt oneself than in the middle of a prank. In the middle, you had to look like you knew how it was all going to come out or it definitely wasn't going to.

Not that this was a prank.

Daffyd rolled his eyes.

Thony started to grin, just to show that he could...

...and then, suddenly, Daffyd's eyes widened... *too* much...

...and everything started *moving*...

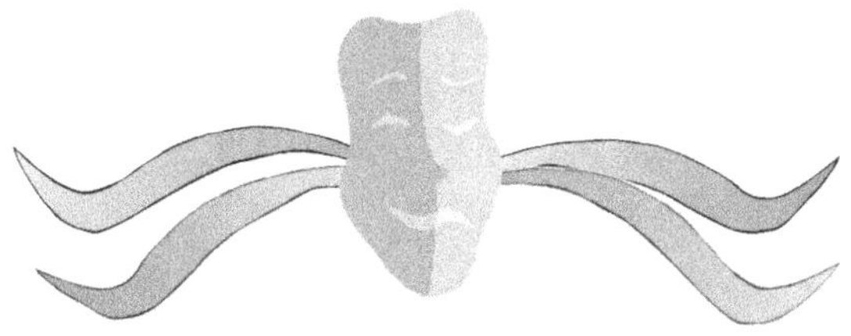

Chapter THIRTEEN

Not the Plan...

IT WAS... *AWFUL.*

Like every nightmare you ever had of *flying* with the highest possible risk of *falling.*

Thony found himself clinging to the buckles of the traces for the last pair of horses that he'd given sugar to. He'd been thrown onto his back on the flat draught-pole as the whole team started moving, and just grabbed for whatever was handy.

Which had happened to be those traces.

There hadn't even been time to scream – or *think* about screaming – before the breath was being crushed out of him and he was holding on for dear life lest he be tossed under all those flashing hooves and crushed...

...although whether the squishy cloud-hills would *actually* allow someone to be crushed to death under lots of pointy hooves would have to remain a mystery, because that risk was suddenly incidental compared to the risk of *falling to his death from a godawful height.*

"Don't look down!" Daffyd shouted, though his voice was being ripped away in the rushing winds.

Not that Thony *could* look down, since he was *lying on his back...*

And just when he thought nothing could get worse...

"Oh my God! And don't... don't look **behind** *us. They're* **all** *coming with!"*

All the crazy-ass flaming horses from the cloud-meadow?

In the name of all the Gods, *why?*

And... it was getting *hotter...*

Which made *no* sense, since they were going *higher* in this *impossible flying chariot.* Didn't the air get *colder* as you went higher?

Aside from Queen Snowmistral's magickally-protected Cloud-Country, that was...

Oh. The horses really *were* flaming.

That... was unnerving as well as hot.

Thony closed his eyes and tried a trick that had sometimes worked to help him hide when he was small. It was kind of stupid – and probably had worked more by chance than anything else – but he didn't have any better ideas and if he was going to fry – or fall – to his death anyways, it hardly mattered, right?

I am part of the flames, he whispered inside his head. *I am just part of the flames. No one can see me, and nothing can touch me or hurt me. I'm just part of what's already here.*

Or okay, when he was a little kid, hiding behind one of Mama's zillions of potted plants, or inside her basket of yarn or whatever, he'd whispered it. He kind of had to *shout* inside his own head just to get over the roaring of the wind and the flames and the neighing of the crazy-ass horses.

He stopped feeling like he was about to turn into a piece of charcoal at least.

So, that was something, even if it was all what a traveling physick that Papa had hired to give Thony and Prissy a few lessons on biology had once described as the 'placebo effect.' Which had seemed to be along the lines of 'if you believe in something hard enough it comes true.'

*(The physick had disagreed with that summation, which had made perfect sense to his pupils since that was about how magick worked. After several, ah, **spirited discussions,** the guy had given up and left, refusing to take Papa's money, saying he was a Man of Science and 'couldn't work in these conditions.' Thony still wasn't sure what the guy had gotten so worked up about. It wasn't like there was an incompatibility between Science and Magick. You needed both to get the world to make sense, after all.)*

Suddenly there was a loud *"WHOA!!!"* in a familiar voice that was very much not Daffyd's.

And something was tugging Thony out of his not-nearly-secure-enough position as the roaring of the winds subsided to something slightly less deafening and the pole seemed to start to –

OH. MY. GOD.

*IT WAS **FALLING AWAY FROM HIM!!!!***

He reached reflexively for whatever was lifting him away, opening his eyes in shock as his hands wrapped around a strong, pale arm and his fingers tangled in the billows of a white shirt.

And then something else white floated across his vision and his eyes closed again just in time to keep... it felt like horsehair... out of them.

The strong arm kept lifting as Thony lost all contact with the chariot's draught-pole, and he was pulled in to be tucked... no... to be *encouraged* to scramble into a pillion position behind some guy and hold on tight...

Well, no question about that last. He was going to hold on until he cut this guy's circulation off or until his feet were back on something solid and stable.

I am safe, I am stable, I am making it back, he told himself over and over. Because, hey, if it had worked with the flaming horse chariot...

A great, friendly laugh erupted from the abdomen Thony was clutching so enthusiastically.

"Look out around us, boy! Ye will not see the like e'er again, mostlike!"

Well, that might be true, but that didn't mean it was something he *wanted to see.*

"Look out," the male voice urged again. "Ye be not a coward, I ken! Not after this little adventure!"

Well, maybe he hadn't been *before* this *mis*adventure, Thony thought, a little resentful of that accusation. But he also wasn't an *idiot,* and one was supposed to *learn* from one's mistakes.

But curiosity *had* always been his bane...

He peered carefully out from the man's back.

On one side of them was a whole *herd* of horses, galloping through the clouds. *(And yes, he'd really just said that. Because he'd seen it.)*

There were herders, too.

Dragons.

Actual, shining *dragons* in a variety of jewel-toned colors.

Thony couldn't be sure, but he almost thought he saw *people* sitting on the shoulders of the dragons as they sloped around, nudging the... herd of cloud-running horses in the direction they wanted them to go.

It was... almost too much. After a moment, the young prince wriggled his head around to peek out on the guy's other side.

The golden chariot was over there, still being pulled along by... good grief, they were cows again. What was *wrong* with those creatures?

It had a driver now, a well-dressed fellow with fluffy, pale golden hair – oh.

Puck.

He seemed entirely in control of the chariot, even confident enough to lean over and talk to someone who was standing beside him holding on to the upper forward rim...

Daffyd.

Part of Thony relaxed to see that his friend was clearly all right.

"Did I tell ye not truly, lad?" boomed the fellow he was holding onto. "Such a sight 'twill likely ne'er occur again. All the Sky-horses let free together at once? What a marvelous day this is – aye, Puck?"

Puck turned and grinned up at them, freeing a hand to give them a thumb's-up.

Somehow, Thony was fairly sure *Daffyd's* expression wasn't *half* so chipper.

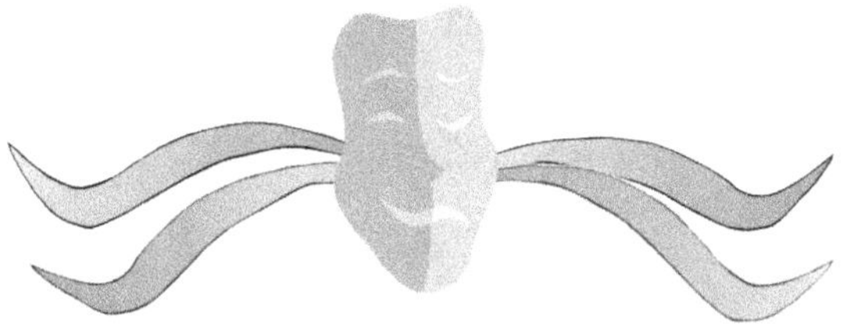

Chapter FOURTEEN

Clearing Things Up?

LANDING BACK IN THE PASTURE meadow on the cloud-hills was a great relief.

Or, at least it was until Thony saw the crowd of *glowing people,* all gesticulating angrily, who were awaiting them.

The rider he was pillion to had his mount circle around while the dragons got the herd of multicolored horses grounded *(or maybe that should be 'clouded,' all things considered)* and Puck brought the chariot in. The cows were horses again, Thony noted absently.

"Ready to face the music?" the rider asked him.

"I don't suppose there's any other choice," Thony sighed. "Well, I guess I'm used to apologizing for pranks gone wrong. How much worse could *this* be?"

The rider's sound of acknowledgment was *probably* a snort, not a snicker.

They were on semi-solid turf a moment later, and the guy helped Thony swing down. His horse – it was that exquisite white mare Thony had noticed before all the crazy began – was several hands taller than the tallest horse the young prince had ever even *seen*, so the help was appreciated.

"You *idiot*," Daffyd ran out in front of the crowd of... *angry Gods?*... and seized him in a tight hug. "I thought you were going to *die!* I thought *I* was going to die!"

He held the rather stunned Thony away from him by the shoulders, and the look in his eye made it entirely unclear as to whether he was about to punch the younger boy in the nose. *(Or kiss him. **Please** not that again.)*

Before Thony could quite decide what to do to pre-empt anything like that from happening, Daffyd pulled him in for another tight hug, muttering things about how Amanita would never forgive him if Thony got killed.

Unfortunately, that interval had given time for the angry Divinities to surround them. The Power and Presence of so many unhappy Gods was utterly overwhelming. Thony began to feel like evaporating on the draught-pole of that chariot might have been preferable. Especially if Daffyd survived.

The only way Thony was still standing was because Daffyd was holding him up and he suspected that the reverse was true as well. And with this much Godliness beating down on them, this mutual leaning thing wasn't going to hold up much longer...

"Hush now," the rider of the white horse stepped close and put an arm around the boys just before they collapsed.

And then he did *something* that felt like having a protective cloak thrown about Thony's shoulders to keep off the rain. It even blocked off most of what the redheaded prince could see of the meadow around them. As well as most of the noise of people – or rather Gods – arguing.

"Are you all right?" Thony whispered to Daffyd, hugging him back with interest.

"I... I think I *will* be," the Pathremiri prince replied shakily. "What the *hell* did you think you were doing?"

Thony sighed. "The... the *sun horses* or *cows* or... whatever they are. They were all tied up and all the other ones were free to graze or get a drink. It didn't seem fair. Or kind."

It was fairly dim inside this... cloak of magick, Thony supposed it was. Or cloak of miracle, because if a God did it, wasn't it technically a miracle? He'd never gotten a clear answer from Prissy or Jo...

Anyways, it was dim, and he couldn't *see* Daffyd's warm smile and rolled eyes, but he could hear them in the older boy's voice.

"Softheart," he was accused gently. "Didn't it occur to you that maybe there was a *reason* they weren't freed? Like, maybe their mistress was coming back shortly?"

"Or that they were too dangerous to run free with the rest?" Thony sighed. "Not until it was really too late... but Daffyd? I'm not sure it would have made a difference to me. I didn't really figure out what those horses *were* until we were airborne. And... it was still *wrong.*"

"Oh, boy," was all Daffyd could say. He hugged the younger boy closer. "I'll... I'll tell Them it was my idea. You just stay quiet and–"

Thony lifted his head and met Daffyd's sad, fearful eyes in shock. "You will *not*. I've always taken responsibility for the things I've done, no matter how they turn out. And *you* had nothing to do with any of it."

"I was in the chariot–"

"Because you were trying to get me to stop doing something stupid. Absolutely not," Thony said firmly. "This was my fault. I get all the credit – or blame."

And that was right when the *cloak* was whipped off of them.

"E'eryone has Their emotions under control now, I think," the Rider of the white horse said in a voice that suggested it had *better* be true. "And there's a few wantin' to ask some questions of you lads..."

Thony pushed Daffyd firmly behind him. "It was my fault. All of it."

A beautiful woman exotically dressed in some narrow sort of gold-embroidered peach gown with pleats in the front and a long, scarf-like part that went over one shoulder frowned at him. Her skin was dark brown – much darker than Daffyd's – Her hair was black and She was wearing more gold jewelry than Thony had ever seen on one person, but it was somehow very *tasteful*. He tried not to look at how Her slender tummy showed between the skirt and blouse of Her gown, or how Her arms were mostly bare, except for about a zillion bangles.

The woman's – Goddess' – arms were folded, and Her black eyes were snapping with irritation.

"We'll apportion blame as *We* see fit, young man. Why were you trying to steal my car?"

Thony blinked in confusion, then realized She meant the chariot.

"I wasn't. Neither of us was."

If he tried to say anything else, it would be taken as making excuses. Thony had all too much experience at this sort of thing; he knew that he had to wait for the right moment to be able to tender an explanation that would actually be *listened* to.

The other Gods had ranged themselves behind the irate and ornate Goddess, apparently seeing Her claim as primary. How long that reprieve would last, Thony couldn't begin to guess. There were still a lot of angry expressions in that crowd.

"How am I supposed to believe you?" the Lady demanded. "My horses say you bribed them with sweets, then climbed aboard and made them fly."

"Now, Ushas," said the Rider, "tha's not *exactly* what they said. Aonbharr and I heard what they told you, too, you know."

She glared at him – but better whatever God it was than Thony or Daffyd. The young princes could still feel the edges of the sizzle of Her glare, even though it wasn't directed at either of *them*.

"Fine," Lady Ushas said. "The horses said that you gave them sweets and offered to free them. And that all the *other* horses wanted sweets, too. And that they took off because you ran out and they wanted more. And because the others were *crowding* them."

She glared around at all the other Gods.

One lovely-but-middle-aged-looking Goddess – who didn't seem all that involved in the proceedings – actually had the temerity to laugh. "This is why I never use animals myself."

Ushas rolled Her eyes. "All very well for You, Alia. You've had the opportunity to build up Your Own story right here on this world. Some of Us are still Bound by the stories begun on other ones."

She rolled Her eyes again. "I mean – symbolism and poetry aside – do you really think I *want* to drive around in a vehicle that can't decide if it's one or a hundred versions of itself or with *cattle* pulling me a percentage of the time? I mean, *cows?* Whose bright idea was that?"

Oh. So... that had all been a Real Thing, not some freakish figment of Thony's imagination.

"Well, at least it's *unique,*" someone else commented, and She turned to glare at whomever had spoken up.

There was a commotion off to one side, and Queen Snowmistral – who suddenly seemed a great deal more serious and majestic and... different in some other way than Thony could explain to himself – came forwards. She was leading Puck and Aleri and the two of them were holding onto a rather frantic-looking Twinklestar. Thony recognized the demi-God of Healing *(and Lies, Politics, and Rogues)* from their sojourn in Flowerdust.

"All is back to normal now, is it not?" Queen Snowmistral said in a cool, confident voice. Thony suddenly noticed that her crown of 'fireflies' was gone and that lightnings zinged around the black stormcloud of Her hair. She seemed taller... and Her exquisite grey eyes seemed to hold all the storms of the world. Or perhaps... even beyond the world, for there was a hint of the birth and death of stars in those eyes.

Lady Ushas turned Her frown on the newcomer. "I still want satisfaction, Sylphara."

The Goddess Sylphara inclined Her head. "A great inconvenience to You, I'm sure, My Friend. But it is surely unnecessary to further disrupt Our celebration over a boyish prank. Allow My Son and Nephew to see that all is made right and the boys receive just consequences for their actions."

"We all know that *Your* Son will only encourage this kind of behavior," Lady Ushas complained.

Puck stepped forwards and bowed – still retaining a hand on Twinklestar, Thony noticed. "I'm sorry for the trouble, My Lady. And You have me to rights, of course. But this devotee of mine–" he gestured to Thony, "–just provided me the strength to complete my last commission for the Guardian of the Ways Between the Worlds. His heart is young and wild – but kind and caring withal. He has been Chosen by this unicorn... and I beg Your permission for the unicorn and my Cousin to see to his care the whiles We discuss matters. Thony has somehow survived close proximity to the Horses of the Dawn so far, but..."

An anguished male voice came from the back. "Let Aleri see to the boy, Ushas. Though it seems unlikely a mortal lad could survive what My Own poor Son could not..."

Lady Ushas looked interested in spite of Herself. "A *boy* with a unicorn... oh, very well..."

Twinklestar bolted to Thony, practically dragging the demi-God of Healing along with him.

Are you okay? Whatever possessed you? I thought I'd never see you again! Are you okay?

Thony couldn't really think around all the words that Twinklestar was stuffing into his head as quickly as possible. He *did* notice Aleri coming in close, pushing them to sit down, and beginning to check him and Daffyd both over.

After a moment, the God of Healing stepped back with a baffled expression. "You're fine. *Both* of you, though I sort of expected that of Daffyd, since the real problems for the charioteer usually start at zenith and you were nowhere near that. Or... even heading there, as I understand it."

The Dawn Horses were trying to get away from the rest, Twinklestar sounded exasperated. *They say you had promised them more apples, and they didn't want to share. What can I tell you? Horses.*

That was clearly an imprecation.

Though Aonbharr is a different sort, the unicorn added reluctantly. Or... reluctantly admiring. Or...

Aleri glared him into silence the way only a Healer can.

"But you, Thony... I'm not sure I can explain you. They tell me you were right in the *middle* of all of Ushas' Dawn Horses. And that they were staying as horses, so I *know* they would have been flaming. By all rights, you *should* have been burnt to a crisp."

Thony wasn't sure if he was being accused of something or asked something.

"I... tried to imagine myself as part of the flames," he said a little hesitantly. "I mean, fire can't hurt you if you *are* fire, right?"

Aleri gave him a measuring look. "That *could* have worked, possibly. If you had practice at it. In a *normal* fire. But *Divine* Fire *should* be another thing entirely."

The Rider had been watching over them as well as keeping an eye on Puck and Sylphara trying to persuade the Others to leave the scene and go back to Their 'celebration.' He seemed to find Aleri's comment interesting, however, and hunkered down beside them.

"Methinks this lad has the touch of Divinity upon him already, Aleri. From whence I know not – 'tis not a touch I am familiar with. But perhaps that is what saved him?"

"Hmmmn." Aleri sighed and shook his head, his face clearing of its concerned frown and being replaced by a look of resigned perplexity. "Your guess is as good as mine, Lord Lew. It's still probably a good thing you got him out of there when you did. I have no idea how long – whatever it was – would have kept protecting him."

Puck came over then, and put his hands on his hips to look down at the boys with the most severe expression Thony had yet seen on the Prankster God. The crowd of grumbly Gods seemed to be headed back to the castle.

"*Please* tell me this was intentional."

Well... that was sort of the opposite of what Thony usually heard associated with that look of disappointed exasperation. He exchanged a baffled look with Daffyd.

"Um, sort of?" the redheaded prince ventured. His friend wisely stayed silent.

Puck sighed. "I *think* I've talked you two out of trouble on account of you belonging to *me.*"

Thony lifted his chin. He was still sort of flabbergasted that he had come away from almost burning to death, but he wasn't going to share blame that belonged to him. "Daffyd shouldn't be in trouble at all. None of it was his fault."

Puck looked rueful. "So, I surmised. I had to claim him the other way – as my grandson. Not that I minded doing that," he added with a fond smile at the Pathremiri prince.

Lord Lew – the Rider Who had saved Thony *(possibly)* – rose to His feet at that. "Your grandson? Congratulations, lad! And who is the lucky lady?"

Puck's face lit up. "Queen Namarina of Pathremir. Daffyd's mother, Ytheril, is our daughter."

"Wonderful!" Lord Lew seemed happy and enthusiastic about *everything,* Thony had noticed. He also seemed to shine with a sort luminescence... much like His steed. "What excellent news!"

The gently glowing God seemed ready to continue in this vein, but...

Okay, Thony was *really* not ready to deal with this.

A *silver dragon* flew up and transformed into a beautiful silvery woman right in front of them. She seemed to carry a sense of entire forests with her, as well as somehow being... *entirely made of flowers?*

Apparently Daffyd wasn't ready for this either, because he started hyperventilating and Aleri had to forcibly calm him down.

"Lew," the silvery Goddess said in a tone of slight exasperation, "what are You still doing here? It's *Your party.* You've had Your fun, but now you need to go be a proper guest of honor. Sylphara shouldn't have to do it all, even if it *is* Her castle."

"If You go with Me, My Love." Lord Lew slipped an arm around the silvery Goddess and kissed her... a rather inappropriately long amount of time.

Thony turned away to give them privacy.

When he looked up again, They were gone.

Puck shook his head and settled down cross-legged on the cloud-hill beside Thony and Daffyd and Aleri. He leaned back on his hands and watched as Twinklestar found a way to kneel down and put his head in Thony's lap without skewering anyone.

"You do get yourself in pickles, Thony," the Prankster God commented.

"Grandfather..." Daffyd asked hesitantly, and Thony could swear he saw Puck wince slightly. "What... Who was that with... with our Goddess?"

Puck's eyes were very kind, though Aleri snorted with a certain dark amusement.

"With *Silvestria?*" Puck asked. "*My* Mother is your Goddess as well, lad."

Daffyd gulped a little nervously, and Puck sighed. "That, grandson, was the Selavani Lord of Light. Lord Lew. He's been looking for Silvestria – under other names – ever since He found this world. Until Lochea was accepted as Mithral's Queen in Selavan They were blocked from finding each other."

"Is he a dragon, too?" Thony asked.

"Not as far as we can tell," Aleri answered. "Although it's... complicated. As things to do with Gods often are. He's somehow been the patron of Selavan without fully being a part of our world. Skiftglow and I aren't really a part of His mythos, so we haven't gotten the whole story yet."

"We – Aleri and I – *think* that Kaliatra – that would be Queen Lilysong to you," Puck nodded at Thony, "was weaving some sort of *connection* between the Goddess that Lord Lew knows on *His* world and Silvestria. Or possibly between *several* Goddesses of His world and Silvestria."

Thony looked at Daffyd to see if that made any more sense to the Pathremiri prince than it did to him. Apparently not.

The two demi-Gods exchanged a glance.

"The details probably don't matter to any of you a great deal," Aleri admitted. "Though the sooner the worship of Lew can make it into the other territories that Silvestria is Bound to, the better it will probably be for all of us. I suspect..."

He winced a little, then shrugged. "I *suspect* that Kaliatra's *intention* is to give Aunt Silvi a reason to be less high-handed with mortals. And... others."

Puck gave his cousin a wry look before turning his gaze back on the boys. "We're not privy to the Grand Plans of the Great Goddess of All. But Her Purpose is *usually* Compassion."

Aleri snorted. "Or *passion.*"

The Snow-Fairy Prince-*cum*-demi-God shrugged. "Tomayto-tomahto, She would likely say. Compassion is one end of the spectrum and passion is the other. Everything in between seems to work for Her as well. But speaking of *compassion...*"

"I think that's *tolerance,* you mean, Cousin..."

"*Whatever.*" Puck gave the Healer-God a reproving look, and Aleri's brief expression of pure mischief made Thony suddenly wonder just how much trouble *these* two had gotten into together over the last few... millennia?

"You've made the Cloud-Country a little too hot to hold the two of you, it seems," Puck continued. "Milady Ushas has *probably* calmed down – Her tempers don't usually continue past a day anyways, since She has responsibilities to see to. Likewise, for most of the rest of the guests. But milord Helios is going to be dismayed that you two survived driving a Sun-Chariot, whereas his own arrogant Son didn't. He's going to want to know *why...*"

"And I don't have any good answers for him," Aleri spread his hands. "I can explain Daffyd – the chariot never got near zenith. But lying that close to the horses..." He shook his head again. "Thony isn't a *God*... or even a *demi*-God. He really *shouldn't* have survived. No matter what 'touch of Divinity' Lord Lew thinks He can sense on him."

Puck nodded. "No one is likely to cause trouble – well, *more* trouble – today, given that celebrating Lughnasadh is the main reason They came together in the first place. But I think we should get the two of you out of here *now*. Aleri?"

The God of Healing – and Politics – nodded. "It's just good sense. They're all – or almost all – solar deities, so if we can keep the boys out of sight until tomorrow, it should *probably* be okay. Aunt Silvi agrees."

Twinklestar, who had stayed quiet the whole time, looked up in alarm at that, making Thony duck and Puck swear.

What about me? And their horses? **We** *can't travel that way!*

"*What* way?" Thony demanded just as Daffyd frowned and asked, "So, *where* are you sending us?"

Aleri and Puck looked at each other, then turned back to the other three with equally wicked grins. "Oh, *you'll* see."

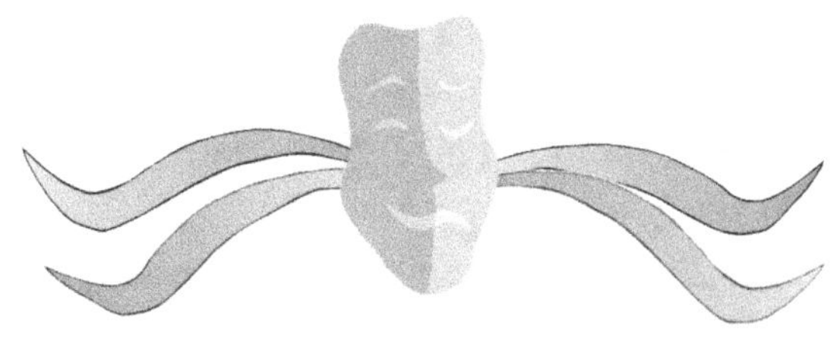

EPILOGUE

(Where Thony and Daffyd Hitch a Ride)

WELL, ONE THING YOU COULD say about Puck and Aleri. Once they made a decision, they acted on it with dispatch.

Thony couldn't help glancing – *again* – at the straps holding his legs in place and keeping him from sliding off into thin air. This was a great deal more comfortable than his *first* introduction to air travel, earlier today... but it was still far too reminiscent of that unintentional ride.

"Quit twitching around," the man sitting in front of him ordered peremptorily. "You're making it harder for Roo to fly straight."

Well, if *those* weren't words to freeze Thony in place for the rest of the trip...

It's not that big a deal, said an unfamiliar voice in his head – which would have made him startle and would likely have gotten him another tongue-lashing from the guy he was stuck holding onto for dear life if he wasn't used to Twinklestar talking to him like this. *Minal worries too much.*

Since *Minal* was the name of the *guy*, Thony had to assume this was the red dragon he was riding on who was talking to him.

Ruby dragon, the mental voice corrected punctiliously. *And my name is Ruserl. Or 'Roo,' to my friends.*

Puck mentioned it, I think, Thony thought back. *I was a little distracted. My first try at flying didn't go so well.*

There was the weird sensation of a mental snicker. *Yeah, I saw. Kesy and I were the ones cleaning up after your mess and herding all those flying horses back to the Cloud-Country. She's the Diamond carrying your friend.*

Thony peeked around Minal's broad back to where Daffyd got to ride the Diamond dragon behind the pretty – and *friendly* – woman. Instead of behind the grumpy guy *he'd* gotten. They looked very impressive against the bright blue sky, though a little hard to look at for very long. The dragon really *did* glitter like diamonds.

Kesyl's dragonkeeper is Diara Torvalds, Ruserl told him, *and you might be better off than your friend when we land. Diara's husband is a little possessive. A pause. And I look pretty good against the blue sky, too.*

I noticed that earlier, Thony told him. *I don't think I even noticed Kesyl, but you were very distinctive... and weren't there some others, too?*

Verenese and Nialan, Ruserl agreed. *She's a Jade, and he's an Emerald. Their dragonkeepers are still pretty young, though. They have a curfew. Minal and I were escorting them back home when we got the call that another dragon was needed again. Kesy can't carry two passengers yet.*

Thony kind of wanted to ask why the Diamond dragon hadn't been with the others, but something in Ruserl's mental tone suggested he really shouldn't. A minor and probably irrelevant mystery, anyways.

There were more important questions.

So, where exactly are you taking us? That was one of the biggies.

Home, was Ruserl's not-terribly-helpful reply. *You'll be safe there. It's under the eyes of too many Greater Goddesses for any other Ones to bother you there. And Aleri says it's really only until sometime tomorrow that you're probably in danger anyways.*

Thony frowned, watching Kesyl cavort a little off to their right. Daffyd and the woman – Diara – seemed to be having a conversation. *He* looked to be having a lovely time.

Well, at least Thony wasn't suffering from altitude sickness, despite being way higher up than before. And Minal's dragon was good company, even if the *man* was kind of stuffy.

The air is right for breathing because of my magick. It's one of the first things we have to figure out before we can carry anyone around. And you have that backwards. Minal is **my** *dragonkeeper.*

There was a certain arrogance to the assertion.

So, you're not his dragon? Thony was a little disconcerted by how the dragon kept picking his not-yet-vocalized thoughts out of his head. *I'm Twinklestar's unicorn-maiden, but he's my unicorn-friend. We're partners.*

Minal *belongs to* **me.** It was said with the sort of finality that suggests a rather extreme exaggeration of facts, and Thony resolved *(very, very quietly)* to ask someone else about this later on. Maybe Diara.

And now he was reminded that Twinklestar was... pretty far away. The connection between them felt... wispier even than it had been when the unicorn had gone away from Flowerdust to meet Quellarie Unicorn-Born and bring her back to help put Shalladra Stillheart in her place.

Puck had said that he'd take care of things, and that Twinklestar and the horses would meet them when they landed. Though it seemed like flying moved you along a great deal faster than even galloping – not that it was possible to gallop from the Cloud-Country to... well, *anywhere.* So, exactly how that was supposed to work was entirely unclear to Thony.

And he still hadn't heard...

And where is your home that we're going to?

Ruserl's mental tone was unmistakably smug. *To Taridawil. The first, best, and most important home of Jewel Dragons in the whole world.*

And apparently, with that, Thony had to be satisfied, since the Ruby Dragon would say no more.

The story continues in
A School for Pranks & Dragons

Book Six of the Prankster Prince
(Book One of Dragons and Damage Control)

Available at online book retailers everywhere in
June 2025

(Need more Prankster Prince stories before that?
Check out the excerpt of
Thony and the Much-Antisipated Adventure in the back of this book...
and/or visit Mangala's website for updates and links to the whole series!)

https://www.RisingDragonBooks.com

MAP
(Daffyd's map that he showed Thony in Selavan)

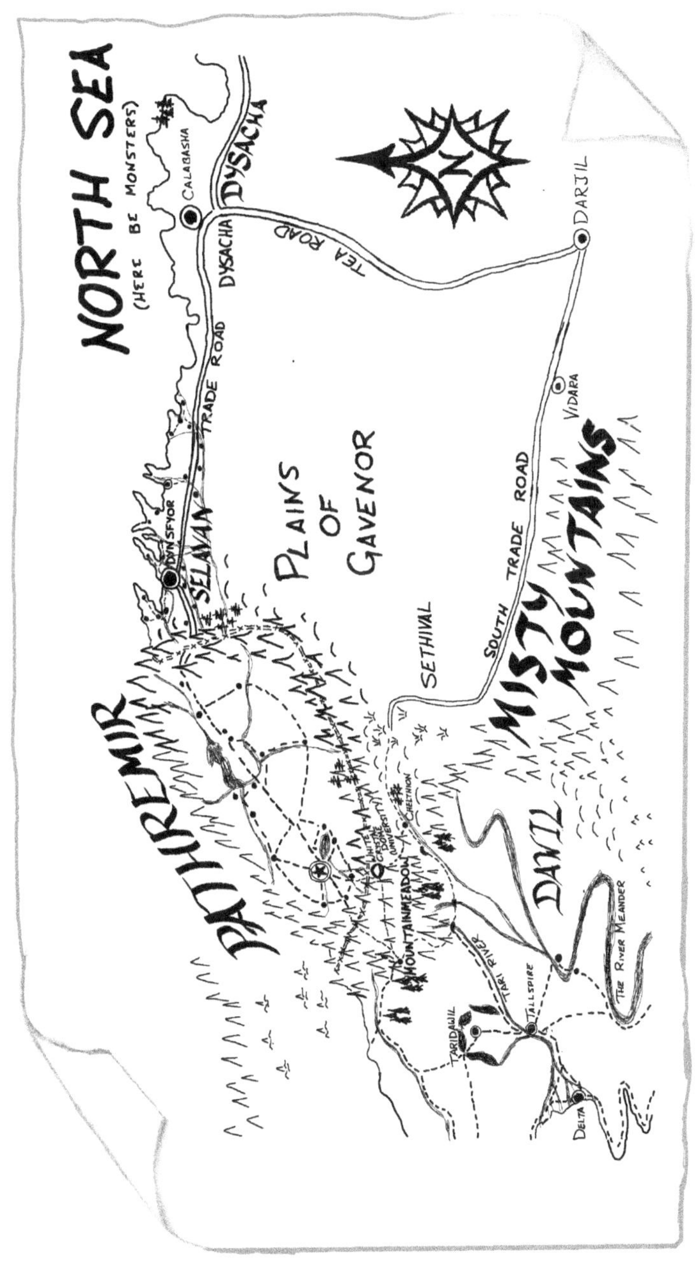

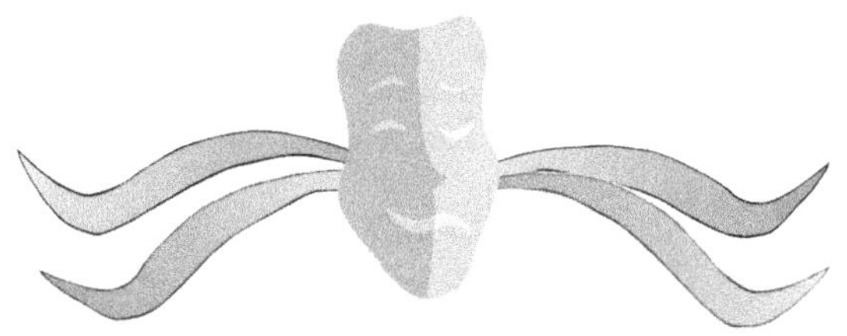

Index of Characters

<u>People in Pathremir at the start of this book</u>

- **Amanita.** Only daughter of the Princess-Heir of Pathremir, second in line for the throne. Daughter of Ytheril and Naeel, granddaughter of Namarina and Skiftglow. Thony's usual companion in mischief and mayhem.

- **Blue.** Street-kid in the Queen's City

- **Daffyd.** Prince of Pathremir. Son of Ytheril and Naeel, grandson of Namarina and Skiftglow. Brother of Amanita.

- **Dell.** Street-kid-chieftain in the Queen's City

- **Divya.** A cousin of Amanita and Daffyd. Daughter of 'fal-Princess Tana.' Ten years old in this book.

- **Naeel.** Prince-Consort to Princess-Heir Ytheril of Pathremir. Father of Amanita and Daffyd. Son of Eldest-Princess Reyalla

- **Namarina.** Queen of Pathremir. Mother of Ytheril, grandmother of Amanita and Daffyd. Beloved of Skiftglow.

- **Nightbreeze.** Daffyd's horse. A black mare.

- **Puck.** (See Skiftglow)

- **Reyalla.** Eldest-Princess of Pathremir. Elder sister of Queen Namarina, mother of Naeel, Falmyra, Tana, and two other daughters. Grandmother of Amanita and Daffyd.

- **Rissa.** Street-kid in the Queen's City.

- **Skiftglow.** Formerly the Puck – messenger, attendant, and general-chaos-causing-problem-solver for Queen Lilysong. Prince of the Snow-Fairies. Son of Queen Snowmistral. Father of Ytheril, grandfather of Daffyd and Amanita, beloved of Namarina.

- **Taeryl** (a.k.a., Taeryllia Avisdatr or 'Taery'). Commander-General of the Pathremiri Armies. A close friend of Eldest-Princess Reyalla. Several adult children by two husbands.
- **Tana.** A 'fal-Princess' of Pathremir. Younger sister of Naeel and Falmyra. Mother of Divya. Daughter of Eldest-Princess Reyalla.
- **Twinklestar.** Unicorn-friend bound to Thony.
- **Thony.** (a.k.a., Prince Anthony Devinthal the Affable and the Affirmative) Crown-Prince of Aldyrwald. Son of King Annabel and King Bill. Brother of Joanna and Priscilla. Unicorn-maiden to Twinklestar.
- **Willow.** Street-kid in the Queen's City.
- **Ytheril.** Princess-Heir of Pathremir, first in line for the throne. Daughter of Queen Namarina and Prince Skiftglow, wife of Naeel, mother of Amanita and Daffyd.
- **Zaja.** Commander of the troupe that Daffyd took to find Amanita.

People Thony encounters in the Cloud-Country

- **Aleri.** God of Healing, Lies, Politics, and Rogues.
- **Alia.** Sun-Goddess of the Muana Desert (far to the south of Pathremir).
- **Aonbharr.** Lord Lew's steed. A beautiful white mare.
- **Bora.** An attendant of Queen Snowmistral. The South Wind.
- **Diara Torvalds.** Dragonkeeper to Diamond Kesyl.
- **Eurosa.** An attendant of Queen Snowmistral. The East Wind.
- Helios. Sun-God of the Greeks.
- **Kesyl.** Diamond Dragon. Her dragonkeeper is Diara.
- **Lew.** Lord of Light of Selavan… and possibly other places…
- **Minal.** Dragonkeeper to Ruby Ruserl.
- **Nialan.** Emerald Dragon.
- **Ruserl.** Ruby Dragon. His dragonkeeper is Minal.
- **Silvestria.** The Silver Dragon Goddess of Pathremir and Dawil, the Lady of Wild Places, the Goddess of Gentle Darkness. Or, as they're now calling Her in Selavan, the Goddess of Light and Dark.

- **Suzarrah Snowflake.** A member of Queen Snowmistral's Court.
- **Snowmistral/Sylphara.** Queen of the Snow-Fairies and mother of Puck. Also – as Sylphara – the Goddess of Winter Breezes, Lady of Blizzards and Gales.
- **Ushas.** Dawn-Goddess of Hinduism.
- **Verenese.** Jade Dragon.

<u>People from the Past</u>

<u>On Thony's Homeworld</u>

- **Annabel.** Queen of Aldyrwald. Wife of King Bill, mother of Thony, Joanna, and Priscilla. Youngest daughter of King Dave and Queen Marybeth.
- **Arabella.** (Deceased) Former Queen of Aldyrwald. Thony's great-great-grandmother.
- **Bill.** (a.k.a. King William). King of Aldyrwald. Husband of Annabel. Father of Thony, Joanna, and Priscilla. Son of King Tom and Queen Lizzy.
- **Dave.** Former King of Silbervale – abdicated in favor of his oldest son, King Joe.. Husband of Marybeth. Father of Queen Annabel of Aldyrwald, King Joe of Silbervale, Prince Tommy, Queen Marybel (of another country), five more sons, one other daughter. Thony's grandfather. He arranged for his seven sons to be turned into swans for Annabel's princess-rescue by Bill.
- **Eddie.** A Knight of Aldyrwald and great-uncle to King Bill. One of (former) King Tom's middleborn brothers. He lives with Thony's family.
- **Esquith.** Thony and his sisters' former tutor.
- **Jeremy.** Centaur stallion, son to herd-leaders Caspar and Mariah. Husband of Priscilla.
- **Joanna.** Princess of Aldyrwald – eldest daughter of King Bill and Queen Annabel, sister of Priscilla and Thony. Also: Goddess of Earth and wife/consort of Roger, God of Air.
- **Joe.** King of Silbervale. Eldest son of (former) King Dave and Queen Marybeth. Oldest brother of Queen Annabel of Aldyrwald. Thony's uncle.

- **Marybel.** Queen of an as-yet-unnamed country. Eldest daughter of (former) King Dave and Queen Marybeth of Silbervale. Oldest sister of Annabel. Thony's aunt.

- **Marybeth.** Former Queen of Silbervale. Wife of (former) King Dave. Mother of King Joe of Silbervale, Queen Marybel (of somewhere or other), Queen Annabel of Aldyrwald, Prince Tommy, five more sons and one more daughter.

- **Priscilla.** Princess of Aldyrwald, middleborn/youngest daughter of King Bill and Queen Annabel, sister to Thony and Joanna. Wife of Jeremy. Also: Goddess of Love and of Animals.

- **Richie.** King of Schwannsberg. Husband of Queen Janet, father of Raymond, Roger, Ryan, Laura, Sophia, and Tessa.

- **Roger.** Prince of Schwannsberg. Middleborn son of King Richie and Queen Janet. Brother of Raymond, Ryan, Sophia, and Tessa. Husband of Joanna. Also: God of Air.

- **Sophia.** Princess of Schwannsberg. Middleborn daughter of King Richie and Queen Janet. Sister of Raymond, Roger, Ryan, Laura, and Tessa.

- **Tad.** Stablemaster in Aldyrwald. A wise and kind man with a great sense of humor.

- **Tommy.** Prince of Silbervale. Youngest son of (former) King Dave and Queen Marybeth. Brother of King Joe, Marybel, Annabel, and six others. His right arm remains a swan's wing as a result of Annabel's princess-rescue.

Pathremiri people from the past

- **Varella.** The first Queen of Pathremir, Amanita's ancestor.

From the Journey through the Fairy Wood

- **Aspenheart.** Prince of the Light-Elves. An attendant of Queen Lilysong.
- **Chillabiaen.** Puck's fairy-steed. A hrulga mare.
- **Girona Starshine.** A student-wizard from the world of Eyola. Cousin to Midele.

- **Lilysong.** Queen of the Fairies. Also: the Guardian of the Ways Between the Worlds (a.k.a., the Waywalker), and Kaliatra, the Great Goddess of All.

- **Midele Featherspray.** A novice priestess of the Golden Sphinx on the world of Eyola. Cousin to Girona.

- **Opalsinger.** Princess of the Dark-Elves. Niece of Shalladra Stillheart. An attendant of Queen Lilysong.

In Flowerdust (or at least that's where we met them)

- **Davril Keetering.** A banker from Selavan. Husband to Istevan, father of Daphne, cousin to Julanna Silversea.

- **Istevan Keetering.** A famous mercenary spy (retired… mostly). Husband to Davril, father of Daphne.

- **Jost.** Former street-kid-chieftain in Flowerdust. Apprentice banker to Davril.

- **Julanna Silversea.** The most famous Bard in the world after her Master Song turned Selavani culture upside down and inside out. Biological mom to Daphne. Former beloved of Valderon Raven'sWing. Cousin of Davril.

- **Quellarie Unicorn-Born.** A half-unicorn woman of great power and wisdom. (She can transform between unicorn and human forms.)

- **Shalladra Stillheart.** A Dark-Elf who tried to take over the Universe with Valderon Raven'sWIng, using the Fairy Wood. Probably dead – she was condemned by Lady Opalsinger.

- **Valderon Raven'sWing.** An (now dead) Evil Wizard who tried to take over the Universe with Shalladra Stillheart, using the Fairy Wood. Former love of Julanna Silversea, biological father of Daphne.

In Selavan

- **Inga Einirsgeld.** A noblewoman who loves books. A friend of Daffyd and Thony.

- **Keeterings.** Madame and Mister Keetering. Davril's parents.

- **Kyrista Keetering.** One of Davril's sisters. A friend of Thony's.

- **Lochea.** Queen of Selavan. Chosen Disciple of the Lord of Light and the Goddess of Light and Dark. Wife of Mithral.
- **Mithral.** King of Selavan. Chosen Disciple of the Lord of Light. Husband of Lochea.

<u>People who are elsewhere but still important for some reason</u>

- **Falmyra.** (a.k.a. Fala) A fal-Princess of Pathremir (daughter of Reyalla, sister of Naeel, aunt of Daffyd and Amanita). Now Duchess of Elaarwen in Ilseador, wife of Duke Eric Alsterling, mother of Rena, Alicia, Celestine, and at least one more daughter. (Ilseador is across the ocean from Dawil... which is to the west and south of Pathremir)
- **Rena.** Oldest daughter of Falmyra. Thirteen years old in this book.
- **Alicia.** Second daughter of Falmyra. Ten years old in this book.

THONY
and the Much-Anticipated Adventure

*Book One
of the
Prankster Prince*

MANGALA MCNAMARA

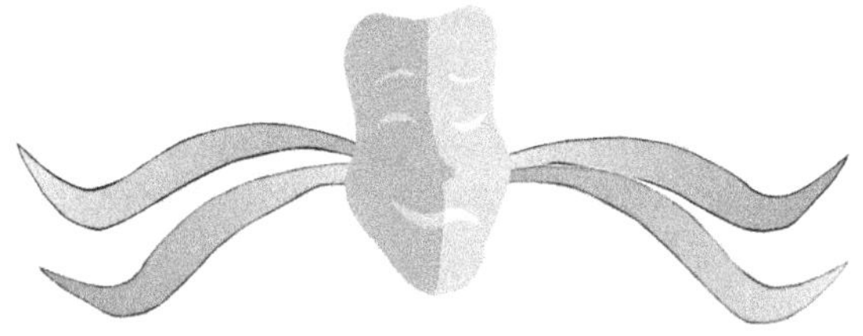

Chapter ONE

A Princely Punch

CROWN PRINCE ANTHONY DEVINTHAL THE AFFABLE (and the Affirmative) of the valley-kingdom of Aldyrwald – an inconsequential kingdom on a substandard continent on an unimportant world –slouched along a corridor of his father's castle, kicking a small rock that someone *(probably him)* had tracked into the castle earlier.

It wasn't *fair.*

His parents were ridiculously overprotective – all because Thony was Heir to the Throne. Queen Annabel had vapors when Thony went out of sight of the castle, even into the *very safe and well-maintained* woods beyond the village. King Bill started to *harumph* and look pale when Thony casually suggested a visit to the next valley-kingdom over, the one ruled by King Bill's best friend who also happened to be the father-in-law of Thony's older sister, Joanna – even *without* Thony hinting that a detour to check out the local giant along the way might be interesting.

Being a crown prince was *seriously boring.*

And anytime he tried to do something to *make* things a little less boring he ended up in trouble.

Today being a case in point.

It was his mother's fault really. She knew better than to come into his rooms.

For goodness' sake, the *servants* knew better than to come into his rooms.

Thony hadn't even been *in* there when Mama had opened the door, taken one look, screamed, and fainted.

Someone had been sensible enough to summon Joanna.

Someone *else* had tracked down Thony and seen him into the throneroom to face his father for a little chat about what King Bill called his 'misdemeanor'. *("<u>You're</u> the one who's meaner!" Thony had yelled in what was, perhaps, <u>not</u> the best display of behavior for a young man who was a few months away from fifteen. No matter that his parents seemed intent on treating him like he was <u>five</u>.)*

So now he was stuck with a fortnight of double-length protocol lessons with Master Eswith – the excruciatingly boring teacher who had reportedly convinced the eternally patient and polite Joanna to threaten to run away from home. *(That was the rumor anyways, passed on from Thony's middle sister, Priscilla. Joanna had been out from under Master Eswith's gentle care years before either of them had begun, though, so how Prissy knew this bit of intelligence was somewhat questionable.)*

An hour with Master Eswith was bad enough and what Thony had to suffer through on a regular basis. By two hours, the young prince was usually falling asleep and the 'gentle master' was beating him about the head and hands with a wooden ruler to *prove* that Thony had fallen asleep and Thony was plotting vengeance on Eswith and whichever parent had stuck him in double-length lessons. The one time King Bill had sentenced him to *three*-hour long lessons, Thony had plotted vengeance on the entire castle.

No one had ever considered doing that again, even though it had been almost five years and he'd grown a bit more of a sense of proportion. Apparently, the memory of caterpillars everywhere – in the bedsheets, in shoes, in the cabinets of clean dishes *(but not in the <u>food</u>. He wasn't an idiot after all)* – still lingered.

168

Thony kind of agreed that he'd deserved what he'd gotten for that one – helping clean up all the mess – but most of his pranks were much more amusing and innocuous. And he still got in trouble with his father over them. *(And <u>honestly</u>? How seriously could you take a man who let his subjects call him 'King Bill'? Thony had long ago decided that if anyone tried to call him 'King Thony' when <u>he</u> was crowned, he'd lop their heads off. Except his sisters. And their husbands; Roger and Jeremy were cool. And <u>maybe</u> his mother.)*

Princes were supposed to go on adventures and do interesting things. Instead, his *sisters* had gone off on The Quest a year earlier – and Left Him Behind. Instead, he'd been stuck *here* in *the most boring place in the Entire Universe*. And with no real hope that he would *ever* get to go *anywhere* or do *anything* interesting. *Ever.*

Of course, he didn't really blame his sisters *(or Prince Roger, the second-born prince from the neighboring kingdom)* for going on The Quest. They'd kind of had to, after the debacle that Prissy's sixteenth birthday party had become. But they'd left him behind.

They'd come back a few months later. Both of his sisters had gotten married while they were gone, though Mama and Papa had insisted that Joanna and Roger, at least, go through a second wedding ceremony *('for propriety's sake' – as if the very fact of Priscilla and Joanna secretly going off on The Quest hadn't taken everything so far beyond the pale of 'propriety' that there was no real way back. But the wedding had made Mama and Papa happier, not to mention King Richie and Queen Janet. Though Roger's older – and as yet unmarried – brother, Raymond, had kept giving both of the newlyweds odd looks as if he <u>wanted</u> to be happy for them, but couldn't quite stop wondering if they were planning to usurp the throne he was to inherit someday.)*

But Joanna had married *Roger*, whom they'd known forever. Mama and Papa were more or less refusing to acknowledge Priscilla's husband at all.

His sisters *(and Roger)* had also come back with the news that their magick-poor world was about to undergo a 'Ragnarök'. All the Gods they had been worshiping forever were about to *die* and be replaced by new ones. And the new ones just *happened* to be: Joanna and Roger and Priscilla – and the handful of friends they had brought back from The Quest.

Oh, and after all that, magick would be much more available to use. For everyone, not just the wisewomen and hermits and witches and sorcerers.

Mama and Papa's skepticism had been palpable. *(No one else than them and Thony had been told about the creation of new Gods at the time, although the word of the 'Ragnarök' had been duly passed along – no doubt with the tale growing less believable with every iteration.)* Princesses falling asleep for a hundred years and princes turning into swans and evil witches and ogres and such were par for the course in their opinion, but *Gods?*

And Joanna and Roger and Priscilla weren't even lucky-numbered children. Joanna was at least an eldest child, but she'd had the bad taste to then have a pair of younger siblings – nine years later, though apparently it hadn't been for lack of effort on King Bill and Queen Annabel's parts at attempting to properly produce three children *(of one gender)* or seven or twelve. *(Or even <u>thirteen</u>, though that number usually created more problems than it solved. King Bill was the oldest of seven brothers, and Queen Annabel was the youngest of seven sisters with three older brothers as well.)*

But Roger and Priscilla were both second-borns.

And then there was Prissy's tail.

Supposedly she'd been born the absolute epitome of perfect princesshood – golden-haired, bright blue eyes *(they were really more green, but for marketing purposes were blue)*, fair skin, the works. But somewhere in the handful of minutes between her birth and being Presented to the Populace, Priscilla had acquired a bushy, black tail that was nearly as long as she was.

When the tail had fallen out of her baby blankets during her Presentation to the Populace – and it was obviously attached to the baby – their father, King Bill, had fainted. *(Which wasn't a <u>manly</u> thing to do, but what can you do when the guy tells people to call him 'King Bill'?)*

Unfortunately, he'd been holding the baby.

Fortunately – despite all the adults frozen in horror around her – nine-year-old Princess Joanna was the only person who had the presence of mind to dash forwards and rescue her baby sister from their falling father. And then to stand up before all the people *(who had been seriously confused, I mean, <u>nothing</u> interesting ever* *happened here)* and declaim that it was a fine tail. That, in fact it was quite likely the finest tail a princess had ever had. And then she told everyone to call Prissy 'Princess Priscilla the Bright-Eyed and Bushy-Tailed' *(which might be where all these ridiculous appellations attached to the royal children had gotten started, though at least Joanna had gotten 'the Wise and Wonderful'. Not that Thony begrudged his sisters theirs, but 'the Affable and the Affirmative'? Yeesh!)* and the poor, confused crowds had cheered enthusiastically.

That was all fine with the Local Populace and even their own minor nobility were willing to go along with things, but Word had gotten out *(Mama said Word always did)* and the royalty in all the neighboring kingdoms had decided the Devinthals had Bad Blood and decided to avoid them. Except for Roger's parents, of course, since King Richie and King Bill had been friends since they were boys.

But since the local nobility of a given valley tended to follow the lead of their king, it meant that all of King Bill's pages and squires were the scions of local families, and all of Queen Annabel's ladies-in-waiting were as well. This was potentially something of a problem, since the girls and boys were sent up to the castle to find a spouse as much as to learn some useful skills, but King Richie had traded them a couple *(which was how they'd gotten to know Roger so well in the first place, though it seemed likely he hadn't been granted permission from King Richie to ask for Joanna's hand – so perhaps even best-friendship only went so far in the matter of Bad Blood)* and if there were somewhat fewer of each group than the king and queen would like, because some of their own more remotely located nobility had sent *their* scions off to other kingdoms, it didn't bother *Thony* at all.

He was busy mulling over all this old history and the Utter Unfairness of having been Left Behind while his sisters had Adventures in the Fairy Wood and how his small attempts to liven up this deadly boring place were met with such an extreme underappreciation... So he wasn't really paying attention to where that rock was going and he nearly tripped over the girl scrubbing the floor.

Well.

Actually, his rock skittered into her bucket and knocked it over, even though he hadn't kicked it all *that* hard.

And *then* this midget-sized girl popped up practically under his chin and belted him a solid one in the gut.

And *then*, while he was stumbling away in surprise, he slipped in the soapy water and fell down, landing on top of the angry girl.

Who called him clumsy and overweight *(which he wasn't, thank you very much, either one. He'd been lanky until a couple years ago and now was sort of... stocky. Priscilla said he was just getting ready for a growth spurt, and she should know if anyone did, since she was now the Goddess of Animals – which apparently included humans, to Mama and Papa's even greater dismay).*

She also called him a thoughtless oaf... and that one struck a bit closer to home, given that he knew that a prince should always be considerate of his People and he really *should* have been more aware of where that rock was going. But he hadn't, because he hadn't been paying attention. Which was sort of the whole problem in a nutshell.

And anyways the whole thing was just too embarrassing. Getting beaten up by a teeny little girl who looked like she was maybe ten – and him almost fifteen? That dinky thing had a right hook that out-sized her for sure! And if he should have to try to explain this to someone...

No. Nope. *Not* happening.

Thony had sloshed halfway down the corridor and almost around the corner when he realized there was something in his *pants*. Something that was *cold* and *wriggling* – and in his *under*pants, or it would have fallen out down his pantleg since Thony didn't hold with hose or tight pants.

It turned out to be a frog and it was alive and relatively unsquished when he got it out... which was a relief, though what he'd had to do to *get* it out in good order had been somewhat embarrassing.

That was when he heard the laughter.

He turned around and saw the scrubbing girl, hands on her hips, and laughing her head off at his antics.

Thony's first reaction was to scowl resentfully at her, but after a scant moment his expression changed to a sheepish grin. He'd stuffed enough frogs down other people's clothes *(though never their underpants* – *and how had she managed to do that without him noticing?)* that he had a fair idea of what he must have looked like. And it *was* pretty funny.

"He's getting away! Help me catch him!" The girl splashed sudsy water as she darted after the frog that was merrily hopping away from them.

Thony followed her without a question. Frogs – as pretty much everyone from Mama to Joanna to Priscilla had informed him on more than one occasion – *didn't* belong in the castle. The stone floors were too hard and dry for a creature that spent much of its life submerged in water, and the servants did too good a job at cleaning even the remotest dusty corners so there weren't enough insects for it to eat. *(Though Mama's concerns were rather different than his or his sisters'.)*

And chasing a frog through the castle together was generally silly enough to make anyone either fast friends or mortal enemies.

Honestly, Thony didn't care which. Either one would lighten the incredible boringness of life in Aldyrwald.

Fortunately, they caught up with the frog just inches before it would have leapt into his mother's solarium to wreak havoc on ladies-in-waiting and embroidery hoops alike.

Not so fortunately, Mama came over to see the commotion at the door, spotted the frog, and fainted. Again.

Joanna was sent for and Thony and the girl were made to wait for her while the ladies-in-waiting waved smelling salts under Queen Annabel's nose and placed cold cloths on her head and gossiped in quiet, giggly voices.

"Twice in one *day*, Thony?" Even Joanna's ever-patient tone sounded exasperated. "What are you trying to do? Get Papa to keep you from ever seeing the light of day again? At this rate even Master Eswith will run out of protocol lessons."

"Um, no...?" She'd phrased it as a question, but Thony had the feeling it was rhetorical.

"And now you're involving the *servants* in your pranks again?" And *that* was disappointment, and if there was anyone whom Thony actually *cared* about not disappointing, it was Joanna.

"It wasn't a prank! The frog just sort of... escaped. And I knocked over her bucket. And then she helped catch it." Which was all true, if slightly out of order. And definitely gave the impression that the frog had been *his* to start, rather than that *he* had been the victim of the *girl's* prank.

There didn't seem to be any good way out of this one. Thony looked at his feet. The girl had the frog, so he couldn't even pretend he was looking at it.

Priscilla bustled up right then – presumably summoned by Joanna in that God-Way they had now, or else called by the frog in her role as Goddess of Animals. She plucked the frog out of the girl's hands and headed back out, cooing at it, and only noticing Thony by way of a quick ruffling of his red curls. She had that look she got when someone interrupted what Thony had nicknamed 'Jeremy-time' – though apparently part of being a Goddess was the ability to appear perfectly turned out in a proper, princessly pink and frilly daygown when one might be seen by one's mother and her ladies.

So much for his best friend since forever.

Jeremy was cool, of course – and how cool was it to have a *centaur* for a brother-in-law? – but Priscilla never had time for Thony anymore.

"The bucket got tipped over? I'd imagine that's how the frog escaped – and why the pair of you are dripping suds," Joanna said thoughtfully after Priscilla had disappeared.

Her eyes looked like she had rather more of an idea of what had happened than that... like she could just look into Thony's own *soul* and pull the truth right out of him. And maybe she really *could*, now that she was the Goddess of the Earth and all. Though she'd been giving him *that* kind of look pretty much ever since he'd first discovered frogs when he was two or three years old, so it might just be a Joanna-Thing and not a Goddess-Thing.

"I should probably get that water taken care of and finish cleaning the floor before anyone slips in it and gets hurt," the girl suggested. Thony decided he needed to remember that little crease between the brows that did such an excellent job of suggesting Concern and Responsibility. Not that it would likely do *him* much good, given that everyone in the castle tended to assume that if there was something crazy going on he was probably the cause of it.

To be fair, they were usually right.

And it was his honor and his privilege to liven things up a little.

174

Even if it did extend those interminable lessons with Master Eswith.

Joanna looked at him with a fair amount of empathy. "I'll tell you what, Thony, you go help this girl clean up all that soapy water and we'll just call it even. I'll make things right with Mama."

That was... not entirely unexpected. Joanna's approach to discipline was all about 'natural consequences', which translated into 'fixing what you'd messed up'. And since cleaning up the messes he'd helped create was *far and away* more interesting than protocol lessons, Thony far preferred it when *she* got to sort him out.

However, he did kind of have to admit that King Bill's approach was probably a more effective deterrent. Not only did it leave the energetic young prince less time to think up new ways to create havoc, but adding to the overall boringness of Aldyrwald – especially in his own personal life – went against every principle he tried to live by.

Though if he managed to stay *awake* while listening to Master Eswith droning on about what fork to use at dinner for which esoteric side-dish that would probably never show up on Thony's plate, he often could daydream up some of his best ideas. Unfortunately, Master Eswith dealt with daydreaming about the same as he did actual sleeping, and bruises from that ruler could really hurt.

"Thanks, Joanna, you're the best!" He stretched up and gave her a kiss on the cheek, then trotted after the girl. She'd taken Joanna's comment as a permission to leave and had almost disappeared around a corner already. He had to move fast to catch up.

Find out what happens next in

Thony and the Much-Anticipated Adventure

Available in eBook, paperback and hardcover at all fine online bookstores!

Or check out the whole series at
https://www.RisingDragonBooks.com/Books/Fiction/
The_Prankster_Prince/PranksterPrince-series.html

Author's Note

Oh, WOW, was this book fun to write!

When I got started, I knew Thony was going to end up running away and that he was supposed to end up in Queen Snowmistral's Court. I had no clue how he was going to get there... or that he would be taking Daffyd and not Amanita. (Though, Amanita has a LOT of catching up to do after having been gone about two years... so I had the sense that she was going to get stuck.)

The rest?

Well, I write to find out what happens!

Describing Queen Snowmistral's Court was fun – Suzarrah (Suzy) Snowflake got a cameo because she's showing up in another book in the Knigtess series eventually, ~~when Karana and Ivan have to fight a war in Chelth~~ I mean... *eventually.*

That... probably isn't a huge spoiler. After all, if Thony is flying to Dawil *right now,* you know he's going to meet Karana and the rest. (But be aware that Thony's stories happen about five years in Karana's future compared to the end of *A Not-So-Sacrificial Maiden...* And choose your reading accordingly. A timeline should be up in the Lore section of my website by the time you read this, to help you decide.)

I actually ended up doing a bunch of research for this one. As you know from my bio, my mom was an international storyteller – I grew up on myths and legends from all over the world, but to get things right (and then tweak them to fit here) I needed to refresh my memory.

As Aleri and Puck sort of explain, there is a connection between our world and this one. It's... a complicated connection, though (as is everything to do with the Gods). As you follow along with this and my other series, you'll come to see what that connection looks like in all its many facets and parts.

Eurosa and Bora (and the other ladies attending on Queen Snowmistral) are female manifestations of the Greek winds. Between the mess the Líonar left in Pathremir and Selavan and how the Pathremiri ended up with their own take on it... there's a reason all the local deities Manifest as female. And it made sense to me that the Lady of Blizzards and Gales might have a close connection with the Greek Anemoi... just for starters.

Helios, of course, drove the sun-chariot for the Greeks before Apollo. He refers to Phaethon, His son who tried to drive the chariot and didn't succeed.

Lord Lew and Silvestria's new(?) Aspect come from the Celtic traditions.

And Lady Ushas is from my own background (my aunt's name was Usha).

I had a lovely time hunting up details about different sun-deities who are involved with horses (more or less). I wish there had been space for all of Them to have speaking parts... but clearly there are Stories to Be Told. Of Their God-get-togethers, among other things.

And, for those of you who noticed Thony ruminating on political organization and peasants – that was a reference to *Plato's Republic*. Because political science and economics are McNamara family passions!

It's gonna be a fun ride!

And – Thony? And dragons? There's a reason why the next book is *A School for Pranks & Dragons!*

(Due out in June 2025!)

See you then!

Mangala

Also by Mangala McNamara

The Chronicles of Ilseador

The Rebel Duchess: Book One

The Prydeen Prophecy Cycle:

 The King's Champion: Book Two

 The Pirate-King: Book Three

 The Pale Sorceress: Book Four

 The UnCaptive King: Book Five

The Heart of Ilseador Saga:

 A Lovely Mess: Book Six

Knightess of the Realm

A Not-So-Sacrificial Maiden

Scaredy Cat:

 A Knightess of the Realm Holiday Prequel Novella

Out of the Woods... Hopefully (a Prequel Novella)

Turns of a Page (A Prequel Story Collection)

The Heir's Journey mini-series (3 books)

 A Not-So-Simple Mission: Book One

 An Entirely-Unexpected Revelation: Book Two

 An All-Too-Surprising Homecoming: Book Three

The Secrets of Dragon Mountain

 An Altogether-Curious Altercations: Book One

 An All-Too-Obvious Choice: Book Two

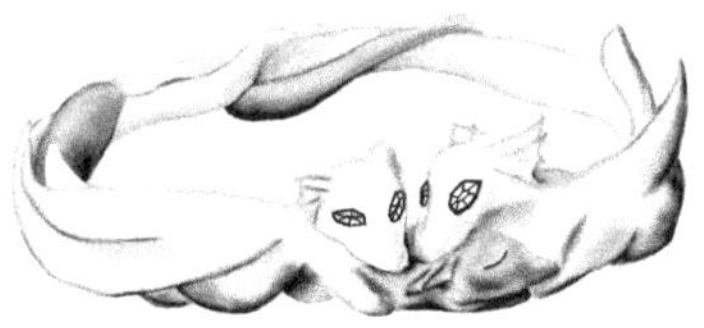

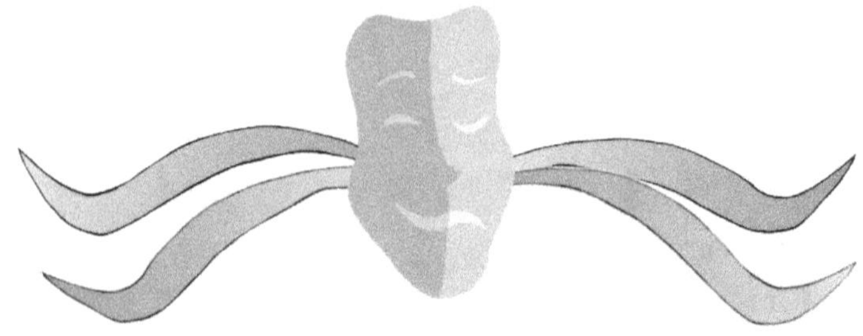

The Prankster Prince

Thony and the Much-Anticipated Adventure

The Raven War Saga (3 books)

> *Thony Goes Astray! (in the Deep, Dark, and Dangerous Fairy Wood):*
> *Book Two*
>
> *So You Want to Be a Hero? Book Three*
>
> *How Thony Stopped a War (and Fixed a Friendship): Book Four*

The Pathremiri Problem (2 books)

> *Diary of a* ~~Runaway Prince~~ *Bold Questing Hero: Book Five*
>
> *A Court of Mists & Misadventures*

And more to come...

Learn about Mangala's upcoming projects (fiction and nonfiction both) and sign up for email updates at

https://www.RisingDragonBooks.com

About the Author

MANGALA MCNAMARA WRITES EPIC ROMANTIC Fantasy. Her Knightess of the Realm and Prankster Prince series occur in the same world as the Chronicles of Ilseador stories.

Mangala lives in Flyover Country (the far northern end of the US South) with her husband, The Professor and three of her six children (the remaining children are in college or grad school). You can blame the oldest kid for the excessive amounts of math showing up in Mangala's fantasy novels, the second one for better attention to staging of scenes, the third for all the economics, the fourth for great attention to history – and all six of them for a focus on political science!

Mangala is a former professional bellydance instructor, and used to enjoy knitting, crotchet and embroidering Temari balls, but now is much more boring as she rarely does anything but write… although she also fences (the sport) and plays boardgames with her kids. She owes her love of books and reading to her mother, who was a professional folklorist and could recite – from memory – stories from every nation in the United Nations.

More Fantasy coming soon…

A n Entirely-Rational(ized) Decision
   Book Three of the Secrets of Dragon Mountain
   (A Knightess of the Realm Novel)
   (available April 2025)

Piled Higher & Deeper
   Book Two of the Heart of Ilseador
   (A Chronicles of Ilseador Novel)
   (available May 2025)

A School for Pranks & Dragons
   Book Seven of the Prankster Prince (Dealing with Dawil)
   (available June 2025)

Visit https://www.RisingDragonBooks.com for more
upcoming books, maps, lore, art, and more!